Holly River Secret

Holly River Secret

by ANN DURELL

Illustrated by URSULA KOERING

Doubleday & Company, Inc., Garden City, New York

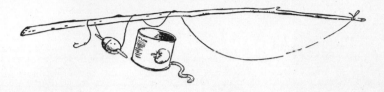

Contents

*To my family
because they once lived at Holly River*

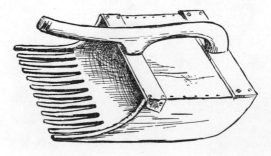

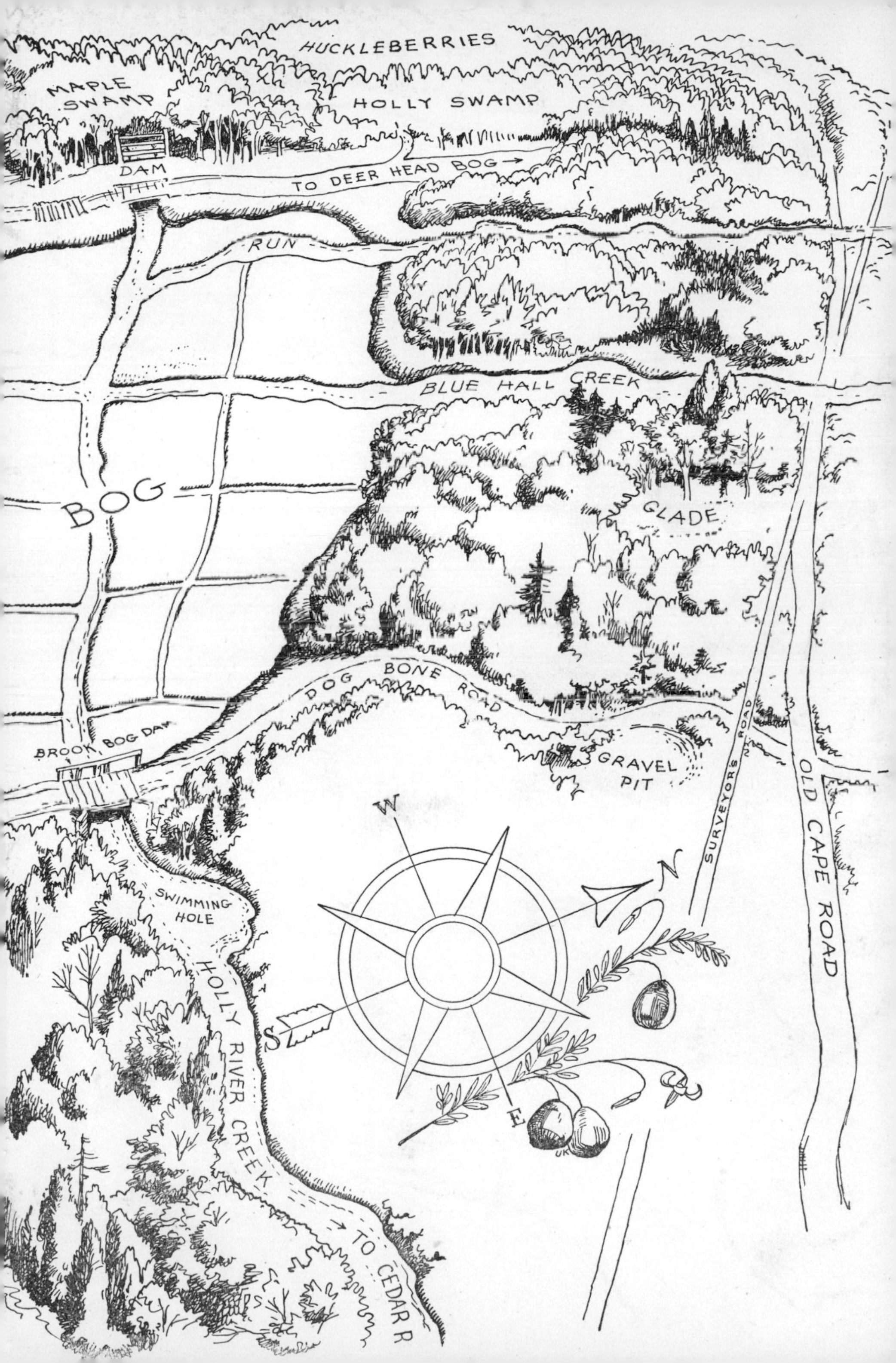
HUCKLEBERRIES
MAPLE SWAMP
HOLLY SWAMP
DAM
TO DEER HEAD BOG
RUN
BLUE HALL CREEK
BOG
GLADE
DOG BONE ROAD
BROOK BOG DAM
GRAVEL PIT
SURVEYORS ROAD
OLD CAPE ROAD
W
N
S
E
SWIMMING HOLE
HOLLY RIVER CREEK
TO CEDAR R

I

Vacation

"Hurry up, Joey," yelled Mac. "Mom's waiting for us."

Joey turned reluctantly away from the group saying good-by to Miss Redding. Next year she would be in the sixth grade in the "big room." It seemed sad to be leaving Miss Redding's room forever after having her for five years.

Sometimes a two-room school didn't seem like such a good idea. Donny and Mac, her twin brothers, were already in the big room, but they were more likely to tease her about being only a sixth grader than help her get used to Miss Miller, who taught sixth, seventh, and eighth grades, and was supposed to be very strict.

"Good-by, Joey," called Miss Redding. "Have a good summer and be sure to come in and see me sometimes next year."

Summer! Joey sniffed the hot air. Beyond the smell of chalk and old wood she could pick up the vacation smells —pine and melting tar, swamp water and gasoline. Fall and the big room seemed too far away to count. Joey hauled her pencil kit and her lunch box out of her desk and hurried for the door. Suddenly she could hardly wait to be out in the sunshine.

"Good-by, Miss Redding," she called happily. "I hope you have a nice summer too."

Mac was teetering impatiently on the steps when she came out. Joey thought of stopping for a last drink of water from the pump by the door, but one look at his red face changed her mind.

"Hurry up," he said crossly. "If we don't get out of here, they'll probably decide to have an extra day of school."

Joey ignored him. "Boy, will I be glad to get out of this old dress," she sighed, flapping her skirt to make a little breeze as she walked toward the car. "I don't think it's fair that I can't wear jeans to school."

Vangie and Evelyn Smith, who were in Joey's class, came giggling by, arm in arm.

"Have a swell vacation, Joey," said Vangie, proudly smoothing the pink lace trimming her best dress.

"My, you'll be lonesome out there on the cranberry bogs all summer, won't you?" said Evelyn pityingly. "It must get awfully dull."

Joey looked at them indignantly. How could anyone think that Holly River might be dull and lonely? She felt sorry for them—cooped up here in Cedarville all sum-mer, with no creek to swim in, no woods to explore.

"I wouldn't spend the summer in Cedarville for any-thing," she said rather snootily.

Vangie rolled her eyes toward Evelyn. "Aren't you scared to death Uncle Tom-Tom will get you, out there in the swamps and the woods?"

"Suppose he came hippity-hopping down the road and you saw his *eye?*" whispered Evelyn.

Joey shivered in spite of herself. She was beginning to

feel scared right here in the sunny playground, but she
was bound and determined not to let Vangie and Evelyn
Smith know it. "I've lived at Holly River for ten years
and I've never seen or heard of any Uncle Tom-Tom."

"Nobody talks about him, that's why. He'll get you if
you even talk about him." Vangie lowered her voice.
"But he lives in the swamps near Holly River, all right,
and he's got the evil eye."

"Cross your fingers when you say that, or he'll come
get you for sure," hissed Evelyn. "Uncle Tom-Tom's eye
is bright red, and if he looks at you he puts a hant on
you."

"What's a hant?" whispered Joey.

"You turn creepy-crawly cold and then you get stiff
as a board and you don't ever move again," Vangie said,
right in Joey's ear.

"Ma'll give you a licking if she finds out you've been
telling about Uncle Tom-Tom," said Evelyn with relish.

Joey pulled herself together. "Nuts! I don't believe
there is any Uncle Tom-Tom. I think you're making it all
up to scare me."

"Just you wait and see!" Evelyn cried shrilly. "He'll
get you for saying that! You think you're so smart, Joey
Finch, just because you live in a big house out at Holly
River and your father came from Philadelphia and owns
a lot of land. You're nothing but a smarty-smart know-
it-all who wants to boss people around. Well, just try
and boss Uncle Tom-Tom!"

She grabbed Vangie's arm, and they flounced away
together.

Joey stared after them, feeling unpleasant. "I'm not
bossy," she muttered. "It's just that I always know the

best way to do things, and it's quicker to tell the other
kids what to do than wait for them to figure it out for
themselves. But suppose they're right about Uncle Tom-
Tom? I'll never be able to go into the woods again."
She crossed her fingers quickly.

"If you don't hurry, Joey, we'll have to leave you,"
called Mom.

Joey ran for the car and scrambled into the back seat
beside Mac. Donny was already hunched up in the front.

"Did you get in another fight?" asked Joey, looking at
his swollen mouth.

"Don't ask embarrassing questions," advised Mom,
starting the motor.

"He was first in his class again," explained Mac. "And
that Maxie Szabronsky said it was because he was the
teacher's pet. So naturally Donny hit him and they had
a fight."

"Maxie Szabronsky is just a dumb Polack," said Joey,
stretching out comfortably. Then she caught a glimpse
of Mom's face in the rear-view mirror and knew she
shouldn't have said that.

"Where did you learn that word, Joanna?" asked Mom,
in her "dry-ice" voice, as Daddy called it.

Joey squirmed. "All the kids call the families that
moved in on the farms at the end of Cedarville
'Polacks,'" she said.

"Well, it's a much more stupid thing to call anybody
than 'teacher's pet,' and I want all three of you to remember that. Anyone who calls another person by a rude
name only proves his own ignorance and bad manners."

Joey sat in chastened silence while Mom steered the
car around a couple of fat hens scratching in the middle

of the street. Cedarville was just one street, lined with rickety unpainted houses, and the Cedarvillers never bothered much about keeping their animals out of the road. There weren't enough cars to make it worth-while.

Joey pressed her nose against the window. She was always afraid she would miss the moment when the last ramshackle place was passed and the dark, swampy woods closed in along the road. Daddy said that their part of South Jersey was true wilderness.

"Have the surveyors come?" Mac asked suddenly.

"Oh yes," said Mom. "They seem to be working pretty quickly. They passed our house about noon."

"Have they proved that Daddy's boundaries were right?" Joey asked anxiously.

Mom laughed. "They can't work that fast. I don't think we really have to worry, though. There wasn't a question of Daddy's boundaries being in the wrong place; he just wanted to have them very clear in case the railroad decides that it needs more land and tries to buy some of his."

"Look!" called Mac excitedly. "There's one of the lines they make. See how straight it is."

Joey sprawled over him, trying to see, as Mom turned the car into the Holly River dirt road, and even Donny forgot his sore mouth and hung eagerly out the window.

"That must be some job, hacking through all those briars," he said admiringly.

"I can't wait to see how they do it," said Joey.

"No one," said Mom, "is to go anywhere near the surveyors. And that's an absolute order."

Mac and Donny groaned, but Joey had crawled over Mac and was hanging out the window.

"John Rufus is going to have a good crop of sweet potatoes this year," she said happily. "I can taste them right now, all soaked in butter and molasses."

"Who cares about sweet potatoes!" snorted Donny. "I hope we get a good crop of cranberries. I wish Dad would let *us* go to work on the bogs."

"He says we can't till we have enough muscle. And if anyone can grow a good crop of cranberries, it's John Rufus," Mac said admiringly. "He doesn't need us. Isn't he a neat foreman, Mom?"

"Yes indeed. I remember your father telling me soon after he bought Holly River and we moved down here that we'd never have raised anything but a crop of briars if he hadn't found John Rufus."

"That was right after you and Dad got married, wasn't it?" asked Joey. She loved to hear the soft way Mom talked about those early days. "I'm sure glad you didn't decide to stay in Philadelphia with Grandmother."

"There was no question of that." Mom's voice wasn't exactly soft now. "Grandmother is apt to think other people must do exactly as she tells them, because her way of doing things is the best. (Joey wriggled. This sounded uncomfortably like what Evelyn Smith had said about her.) Dad had been offered a job teaching in a university near Philadelphia, and Grandmother wanted him to take it so that she could keep on managing his life. But because her way isn't Dad's way he decided to come here where he could run things to suit himself— and me! Besides, he'd already seen Holly River on a deer-hunting trip and knew he wanted to live here and raise cranberries."

Joey had never heard this story before, and she wasn't

sure she liked it. She was beginning to sound too much
like Grandmother.

They were driving over the House Bog dam. The bog
was still like a lake, lapping against the brushy banks
holding in the water that protected the delicate cranberry vines from cold all winter long. But Joey could
hardly wait for the day when John Rufus opened the
gates in all the dams protecting Daddy's bogs and the
brown water rushed to join the swamp water lazing
down the little runs. And the runs would empty into
Holly River Creek, and the creek would flow into the
Cedar River, and the Cedar River ended with the tides
of the Atlantic Ocean. Someday Joey wanted to follow
that dark and secret route through the swamps that their
water took to the sea.

"I'd probably be eaten alive by the mosquitoes on the
way, though," she thought as she slapped a big one
settling for a meal on her arm.

It would be fun to have the water off and see the bogs
looking like bogs again, with the vines matted thickly
along the bottom and the berries on them turning red in
the sun.

"When's John Rufus going to let the water off the
bogs, Mom?" she asked.

"You'll have to ask Dad," Mom said, swinging the car
into the driveway. "I've been too busy baking to worry
about the bogs."

"Sticky buns?"

Mom nodded.

"Yippee!"

Joey ducked quickly as Donny and Mac hurled
themselves out of the car, and then streaked after

them into the kitchen. She knew better than to get between the twins and food.

The sticky buns were warm and chewy. The butter trickled out with every bite to mix with the maple-syrup topping.

"Ah," sighed Joey.

Donny and Mac just buttered and chewed, chewed and buttered.

"No more," said Mom finally. "I want everybody to be reasonably hungry for supper. Grandmother's coming, so we'll have stewed chicken and peach shortcake."

"Grandmother! We'd better get out before she gets here. If she catches us she'll keep us around all afternoon. What do you bet she'll ask us to 'speak your closing day recitations'? Where's my fishing pole?"

"Boy, it sure is a good thing we fixed our tackle last night."

Joey watched Mac and Donny prepare to light out. They always left her out of their projects unless she could think of something better for them to do that included her. She thought hard but nothing came. A dull afternoon loomed in front of her, but for once Grandmother came to her rescue.

She appeared right there in the kitchen door, and you would have had to be a lot braver than Mac and Donny to walk past her.

"Why, Mother Finch!" Mom put down the plate of sticky buns and hurried over to kiss Grandmother. "I didn't hear you come in."

"That's no wonder, with all this shouting. Good afternoon, children."

"Hello, Grandmother," chorused Joey, Mac, and Donny politely.

"Louise, I shall never understand how you endure living in the midst of constant bedlam. Donahue, your face is smeared. Mackenzie, I am happy to see, has at least attempted to wipe his. And how gratifying to find Joanna in a skirt, even though it is sadly crumpled."

Mom looked cross. She didn't like it when Grandmother caught them looking messy. Probably because of Grandmother's not wanting Mom and Dad to come to Holly River in the first place. Grandmother was always predicting that the children would grow up to be savages, living way out here in the country.

Dad lost his temper once and asked Grandmother what in blazes did she mean by "savage."

"Unruly and superstitious," had snapped back Grandmother.

"I'll grant the children are unruly at times," Dad said rather grimly, "but they've never listened to the absurd stories about 'hants' that the Cedarvillers like to frighten themselves with, and, believe me, they never will."

"Humph!" said Grandmother, which meant "just you wait and see."

Joey came back to the present with a start.

"Why don't you all go and get out of your school clothes and wash up?" Mom was suggesting. "I'm going to make Grandmother a cup of tea, and we won't need you for that."

"Yes, I would like a cup of tea and a little rest," said Grandmother. "Those roads from Philadelphia are worse each time I come. James does his best, but the bumping is torture for me."

James was Grandmother's chauffeur.

Joey started to sneak quietly toward the door.

"But I'll expect to see you children later on. You have probably learned recitations for the last day of school. You can speak them for me after I've rested."

She marched off toward the living room, and Joey raced for the stairs. She had to get out of this scratchy old skirt first thing.

When she joined Donny and Mac in Donny's room she had on the same outfit they did. Blue jeans, cotton shirt, and sneakers. They were sitting on the floor looking glumly at their fishing tackle.

"She'd see us if we tried to sneak out with it," Mac said finally. "You can't hide a bamboo pole under your shirt. 'Where are you going, boys? Come and speak your pieces!' Gosh!"

Joey hung out of the window and watched James polishing Grandmother's big black car. It looked pretty silly on the dirt road in front of the house.

"I thought I heard a dog," she said. "Didn't Daddy take Maybelle and Wolf to the vet's?"

"What a dope. That's Grandmother's Baby. James has her locked in the car."

"How could you think that dachshund's yip-yip sounded like a police dog or a setter barking? Girls!"

Joey didn't pay any attention. She was used to being sneered at. Besides, she had an idea.

"Why don't we do a pretend?" she suggested.

The boys looked interested. They still liked to act things out when there was nobody around to laugh, and nobody could think up more exciting pretends than Joey, although they would have been the last to admit it.

"Cowboys and Indians?" asked Mac.

"No," said Joey. Her idea was beginning to take hold. "Moses in the bulrushes."

"That old thing! We've played it a hundred times. I'd rather go dig worms." Donny picked up his tin can.

"But listen," said Joey. "We could use Baby for Moses."

Mac joined her at the window. All three of them had had to take turns "walking" Baby. She seemed to enjoy slipping her wormy little neck through the collar and getting them in trouble by hiding until Grandmother herself had to come out and call, "Come, Baby!" several times. Not even Baby could hide from Grandmother.

Donny strolled over and the three of them considered. Joey could feel her idea catching on.

"Hunkers on Pharaoh," said Mac finally.

"I know just the costume for you," said Joey. "Come on up to the attic."

Joey didn't like to go up to the attic as a rule. She didn't like the narrow stairs that you couldn't see up or the big black caves under the eaves where the trunks were. But Mac and Donny got rid of all the scary things. Except the wasps. They zoomed around like little airplanes, but if you ignored them they didn't sting. She headed right for the dress-up trunk, which was at the top of the stairs, and in fifteen minutes the three of them were on their way out with great bulges under their shirts.

"How are we going to get Baby away from James?" asked Mac as they paused to scout in the shrubbery by the front steps.

"That's easy," said Donny. "We just tell him Grandmother told us to take him for a walk."

James looked a little suspicious, but he handed Baby right over. Joey thought he was glad to get rid of that awful yip-yip. Baby didn't like being shut in the car.

Holly River House was like an island surrounded by bogs and swamps. Swamp behind the orchard and the garden in back, beyond the road in front. House Bog beyond the Indian-grass field on one side. Brook Bog beyond the gravel pit and the garage on the other side. And the only way off the island was over three dirt roads that led over three dams. One road past the House Bog to Cedarville; one along one side of the Brook Bog to the packing house and the other bogs; and one around the end of the Brook Bog to the old Cape Road. By common consent the twins and Joey

started over the dam toward the old Cape Road, break-
ing into a run just as soon as they were hidden by
the trees.

Donny carried Baby. Of course, she started to yowl
when the running commenced, so he wrapped one end
of the Captain of the Guard's robe around her head.
They always added a wicked Captain of the Guards
to the Moses story because that made the right number
of exciting characters.

"Keep going," Joey panted. "We don't want James
to smell a rat."

They spurted ahead so hard that Mac got a stitch in
his side and had to flop down by the gates that regu-
lated the flow of Holly River Creek through the dam.
Joey lay on her stomach with her head over the side
of the dam, studying the gates, which never failed to
fascinate her. They were like a wall of boards across
the gap through which the creek flowed. When John
Rufus came to let the water off the bog he would take
some of the boards out and make the wall shorter, so
that more water could rush out.

Joey dropped a stick in the bog and watched it wash
over the top of the wall and rush away to the sea.

"How do these old gates last so long?" she asked idly.

"Because they're cedar," Mac said. "Thick cedar
boards will last for years."

Donny was having a hard time keeping the squirm-
ing Baby muffled.

"Let's go!" he said.

Mac decided his stitch was gone, and they slid down
the side of the dam away from the bog, one at a time.
Then they were beside the swimming hole, where the

creek widened before it entered the swamp. Joey squatted down and began to pull her costume out of her shirt front.

"I see old Granddaddy Pike," she teased. The twins were always trying to catch that pike that nobody else believed existed.

"I see a big black snapping turtle," countered Donny.

Joey jumped. She was scared to death of snappers.

Donny had tethered Baby with his own belt to a handy tree, and was getting into his costume, an ancient red-and-gold brocade bathrobe. Mac's robe was only blue serge, but as Pharaoh he also wore an old hooded cape which was red as a holly berry and the best costume they had. As Princess of Egypt, Joey trailed a purple velvet evening coat of Grandmother's, whose chief glory was its clusters of marabou feathers.

"Where's the basket?" Donny asked impatiently.

Joey produced it proudly. She had spent a whole rainy afternoon lining the old clothespin basket with oilcloth and canvas and carefully calking it to make it waterproof.

"It really floats. I tested it in the bathtub."

They swaddled Baby and tied her securely in the basket. Then Mac and Donny concealed themselves in a clump of pussy willows, and Joey in her dual character of Miriam, sister of Moses, set the basket afloat on the black surface of the creek.

"Oh, little brother," she moaned loudly, flapping her hands, "what will become of you?"

"A-r-r-h!" snarled Baby shrilly.

"Joanna!" Grandmother's voice had never carried more clearly or sounded more awful. "What are you doing to Baby?"

Joey looked over her shoulder. Grandmother was standing on the dam glaring at her.

"Retrieve Baby instantly," she called.

Without a moment's hesitation Joey plunged into the dark water and paddled out to the basket, which was rapidly being whirled beyond reach. The purple coat floated out behind her. A snort of laughter came from behind the pussy willows. Mac and Donny would probably have escaped back into the swamp and cut safely home if they hadn't been mean enough to laugh.

"Mackenzie and Donahue, come out instantly."

The boys emerged, still shaking, but under Grandmother's look they sobered up enough to help Joey flounder ashore, basket and all.

They straggled home practically in silence.

"The basket would have caught on a snag before it went very far, anyway, Grandmother," Mac ventured once. He could usually get away with more, because he had Grandmother's family name and red hair.

Grandmother remained grimly silent.

Daddy's car drew up beside the house as they marched into the front yard. They must have looked pretty funny, still in dress-up attire, with Joey dripping purple dye at every step, but he didn't laugh.

"Take your mutts," he yelled. "The vet gave them a clean bill of health."

Joey forgot about being in disgrace when she saw Wolf leaping toward her. He was a huge Alsatian that Daddy's friend, Mrs. Lindley, the county librarian, had found wandering the streets of Cape May Court House, the county seat, and teased Daddy into taking home. Wolf had arrived shut in the back of Daddy's car, snarling and growling. He had taken one look at Joey, who was very small then, and the growls changed into a friendly whine. He stuck to her heels like glue from that moment on. Daddy thought Wolf must once have been a police dog and liked protecting little girls. Anyway, Joey could explore where she liked, as long as she had Wolf with her.

Maybelle, a floppy English setter, was trying to turn herself into two dogs in order to lick Mac and Donny simultaneously.

"Maybelle may never have won a show," Donny had said once, "but she could take first prize for being the dumbest dog in the world." But let anybody else say that!

Daddy kissed Grandmother. She handed Baby over to James, who looked as if he had gotten a good scolding already.

"Louise!" Daddy called.

Mom came around the corner of the house balancing a basket of clothes she had just taken off the line. May-

belle, overcome with joy at seeing her again, bounded on
her happily. Down went the clothes into the dusty
driveway.

Mom stood and looked at her clothes, at the muddy
twins, at dripping Joey.

"Louise," said Grandmother, "these children must be
moved to Philadelphia before they become any more
savage."

"I think," Mom said grimly, "that I agree with you."

Joey shivered with apprehension.

2

Joey Finds the Glade

JOEY woke up the next morning feeling as if she had eaten a bowlful of misery before going to bed, as John Rufus would say. Or limburger cheese! They had all eaten that after one of Grandmother's fancy dinners, once, and Joey felt just the same when she got up the next day—not exactly sick, but with a nasty twisted feeling in her stomach.

She lay and looked at the fat dragon which a long-ago leak had marked in the ceiling over her bed.

"If we go live with Grandmother I'll have that room with little blue dots all over the ceiling," she thought. "And every single morning when I wake up they'll make my eyes hurt."

Joey had never forgotten the dreadful Christmas when Mac and Donny had the measles and she was sent to stay with Grandmother until they were out of quarantine. Besides the little blue dots there was Hannah, Grandmother's maid, who buttoned Joey into a stiffly starched dress every morning and combed her hair into braids so tight that they gave her a headache.

After breakfast, with Grandmother saying "Break your toast into small pieces before you butter it" and "Only *one* spoonful of sugar on your oatmeal, Joanna," there was a long, dreary walk. Joey loved walks, but not down gray city streets on cement sidewalks with Hannah, who talked about how much her corns hurt her. Joey thought anyone who had to walk on concrete every time she stepped out of the house was bound to have corns.

In the afternoon there was nothing to do except keep quiet while Grandmother had her nap. That meant sitting on a velvet chair that scratched the back of her knees and reading a long, dull book about Elsie Dinsmore, whose father was much more like Grandmother's son than Dad, or putting together a jigsaw puzzle. Paints "might spill on the carpet" and paper dolls "were not educational."

And then there was the tapioca and prunes for supper and going to bed alone and hearing the scary city noises outside the window.

Joey jumped hastily out of bed and prowled around her beloved room to make sure she was still there and not in Philadelphia.

"If staying in Holly River means I'll grow up to be a savage, then that's what I want to be," she whispered fiercely.

Imagine leaving the crammed toy chest with its comfortably padded top; the doll house, built right into one end of the long, low bookcase; and the big sunny windows with their easy access to the grape arbor via the back porch roof!

She began to scramble into her clothes. Good old dungarees and shirt. It was a lucky thing Grandmother had gone back to Philadelphia last night, because otherwise it would mean another day in a dress. Last evening had been terrible, all right, with Grandmother telling

everybody off, even the grownups. She had followed
Dad right into his study when he had gone off to do some
work after dinner, and talked and talked. Then Dad
called Mom in, and when she came to send them to bed
she looked terribly sad.

That was the worst about being bad, Joey reflected.
You couldn't tell if what you did was going to turn out
to be funny-bad or wicked-bad to the grownups. Nor-
mally Dad and Mom would probably have laughed at
the idea of Baby floating down the creek in the clothespin basket, but with Grandmother here it turned out to
be the last straw and would probably end up getting the
three of them sent off to Philadelphia.

"Hot cakes and sausage!" Mom's voice and the warm
smell of frying sausages floated up the stairs. There was
a crash as the twins hit the floor simultaneously in the
next room. Joey yanked the covers up on her bed and
smoothed down the spread. As she sprinted into the hall
she nearly collided with Dad, who was buttoning his
shirt as he hurried for the stairs.

"Hot cakes certainly make a good breakfast bell," said
Mom, looking around the table five minutes later.

Joey took a long drink of milk. "I can never decide
which I like better," she said, "hot cakes or blueberry
muffins. Right now I'm sure it's hot cakes."

"And next time we have blueberry muffins they'll be
your favorites," Donny said scornfully.

"What's everybody going to do today?" Mom asked
quickly.

"I'd sort of like to follow Holly River Creek a way. We
haven't done that since last summer, and then we didn't
get very far." Joey looked hopefully at the boys.

"Donny and I are going to try the fishing in that little creek way up at the Deer Head Bog," announced Mac firmly.

Daddy handed his plate over for more hot cakes. "Before you boys start making any long-range summer plans," he said, "I'd like to discuss the possibility of your working on the bogs. I'm sure you could use the extra money, and I need a couple of extra hands."

Mac and Donny beamed. Dad had always said they couldn't work on the bogs until they had enough muscle to do a man-sized job, and now he was saying they did.

"If you decide to do it you'll have to work the regular hours," he said warningly. "No taking off for an afternoon's fishing except on Saturday and Sunday. And no quitting in the middle of the summer because you've found something you want to do more. You'll be treated like responsible workmen, and you'll have to act like them."

"That's okay with us, Dad," Donny said seriously, and Mac nodded too. "When can we start?"

Dad looked at the National Fertilizer Company calendar hanging over Mom's head. "Today is Friday," he said thoughtfully. "You may as well work the half day tomorrow to get yourselves broken in. That will give you Sunday to rest your muscles. And don't think they won't ache!"

"Oh boy!" Mac flexed his proudly.

Joey stared miserably down at the last soggy cold pancake on her plate. There was no one for her to do things with except the twins, and if they were going to be working all day she'd be all alone. Even on weekends they would be busy getting caught up on their private proj-

ects. And the worst of it was that since Evelyn and
Vangie Smith had told her about Uncle Tom-Tom and his
evil eye she was afraid to go in the woods alone, even
with Wolf for protection. It was beginning to look as if
her vacation wasn't going to be any fun at all, and she'd
probably have nothing to look forward to at the end of
it but a hideous winter in Philadelphia, if Grandmother
had her way. She got up and gloomily began to clear the
table.

Mom looked at her sympathetically.

"Why don't you take Wolf and explore the surveyor's
lines, Joey? They finished this section yesterday so you
wouldn't be in the way."

Joey stared intently at the butter. If she admitted that
she was scared to go off alone she would have to explain
why, and once she started telling about Uncle Tom-Tom
there was no saying where it would end. One of the
things that were going to make them savages, according
to Grandmother, was Superstition, which meant Uncle
Tom-Tom. But if she told Mom about Uncle Tom-Tom,
just hearing Mom say that Vangie's stories were Superstition and Joey would be better off in Philadelphia
wouldn't make the swamps and the woods one bit less
scary. Here in the sunny dining room it was easy to say
that there was no such thing as a hant or an evil eye, but
out in the shadowy, rustling woods it was a different
story. On the other hand, she really did want to see the
surveyor's lines.

"I guess I will do that," she said, heading for the pantry
with a pile of dishes. Beulah, who was one of John
Rufus's nieces and who came in every day to help Mom,

was there already, clattering the dishes through the dish pan.

Mom came through after her and began to make out the shopping list.

"Did you make your bed?" she asked.

"Yes," said Joey, thinking a little guiltily of the lick-and-a-promise job.

"Well then, run along."

Wolf, who was not allowed in the dining room, was waiting as usual in the front hall. Maybelle had already left this post to join the fishing party. Joey snapped her fingers at Wolf, and he unfolded lazily and padded after her, his nails scratching faintly on the wood floor.

Outside the sun was very hot, and Joey had to screw up her eyes after the dim hall. A fresh east wind was blowing, and in it, mixed with the cedary smell of bog water, she could scent the salty dampness that meant rain was coming soon. She thought for a minute and then headed for the dam along the Brook Bog. She couldn't help chuckling as she passed the scene of Baby's impromptu voyage, but the chuckle died abruptly as the trail wound into the woods and the rustling shadows closed around her.

"It sure is nice to be out of the sun," Joey said, and then wished she hadn't spoken so loudly when the words died away, leaving a bigger, lonelier silence than ever.

Wolf wasn't much help because he got excited in the woods and was forever racing off after some smell or other and then somehow crashing up behind her and scaring her more than ever. Joey marched along, trying to enjoy the endless stretches of oaks and pines, the gay twitters of the birds. Daddy had told her once that the

Lenni-Lenape Indians came down through these very woods on the way to the seashore and a fresh supply of wampum. Joey decided to pretend that she was Snow Flower, sister of King Nummy, last of the Indian chiefs in Cape May County. Swift as any of the warriors, she followed her brother in the single-file trek through the forest on silent moccasined feet. Ah! A deer! In one motion Snow Flower had fitted an arrow to her bow and raised it to her shoulder. Zing! A bull's-eye! Humble and admiring, the braves gathered around, praising her wonderful skill as a hunter. C419062

Crash! A branch thudded to the ground nearby, and Joey-Snow Flower jumped. Suppose—just suppose—she turned her head and saw Uncle Tom-Tom hippety-hopping up the road behind her with his black coat flapping and his one eye glowing like a big red coal.

She turned her head, and there was nothing on the road. Joey stuck her chin out at her own silliness and plodded on. She rounded a corner and came upon the old gravel pit which meant she was nearly to the Cape Road, so she began to use her eyes. If she didn't, she'd go right by that surveyor's line. Only a few yards on she found it, a long path cutting diagonally across the trail she was on, as straight and as narrow as an arrow. Joey stepped on it, and after some thought decided to go left.

"That way I'll hit the Cape Road farther down, and I can circle around and come home by way of the Blue Hall Creek," she thought.

Wolf returned from an excursion to bark at her sharply. He didn't like this queer new trail at all. Joey hesitated again, for she usually followed Wolf's warnings. He had good reasons for them. But the sun was bright on this freshly cleared path, and she was really curious to explore a new section of the woods.

"Come on, Wolf," she ordered crossly and plunged ahead.

Gradually she began to have the awful feeling that she was being followed. The snap of a twig, the frightened flight of birds, the creepy sensation of eyes (or eye!) fixed on her back. And then she found the Glade and forgot all about it for the moment.

It was like entering another world. One minute she was fighting through briars and scrubby bushes, and the next, she was walking easily on long, silky, green grass, under big elm and walnut trees. Joey felt as if she was in a storybook. She walked across this wonderful clearing, her mouth hanging open, when suddenly she stubbed her toe and fell flat on her face. When she managed to get up she looked eagerly around. Rocks were practically nonexistent in Cape May County, but she had certainly stumbled on one then. She soon found it, camouflaged by the long grass, not a rock but a brick!

"Somebody had a house here once!" The thought popped into her mind before she knew it was coming.

There couldn't be any other way to explain that brick, unless once someone had used this clearing as a dump. The Cedarvillers did awful things to the woods with their trash. Joey had seen Daddy go off like a firecracker over some tin cans they had come across on one of their walks. But somehow this clearing didn't have any connection with Cedarville, or Holly River either, for that matter. It was more like a book place, something out of the olden times.

"I can't imagine what a house would be doing right

spang out in the middle of the woods, though," Joey told Wolf. He flopped down and closed his eyes as if it tired him just to think about it.

Joey shut *her* eyes and tried to see the ruins of an old burned-down house near school that she and Mac had explored once. Just the line of four walls and piles of black bricks. . . .

She banged down on her knees and started scratching like a hungry hen with fourteen chicks to feed. Wolf, charmed with such frenzied activity, began to dig too, only he was looking for a mole or a woodchuck. The earth flew so hard that Joey got some of it in her eye and had to sit down and cry it out. And what did she sit on but a big sharp brick!

"Ow!" she yelped, "this proves there must have been a house here. This brick is in a straight line with that other one. I bet if we kept on we could find just where the walls were, Wolf."

But Wolf wasn't listening. He was down on his stomach with his ears back, growling, not his let's-play growl, but a low, nasty one that didn't seem to be coming out of him at all. The skin on Joey's neck started crawling up her scalp, but that was all of her that would move. Her legs plain gave up from fright. Behind a sumac tree, on the other side of the clearing, a branch snapped. Then two distinct footsteps sounded on the dry leaves, as if someone had lost his balance stepping on a branch and quickly tried to regain it. And it wasn't birds or rabbits, but something with two big shoes on. Joey knew that as well as she knew that she was squatting there like a scared possum, with her eyes glued to the sumac tree. She knew what shoes sounded like when they came

down on dry leaves, even though she couldn't actually see anything.

Then Wolf sprang to his feet with a loud bark and charged across the clearing, raising enough rumpus to be heard out in Cedarville. Joey didn't wait to see what he flushed from behind that tree. She took off at top speed in the opposite direction, crashing through the briars as if they were spider webs. And the next thing she knew, one of her questions was answered, for there she was on the Cape Road. It had been a few yards from the clearing all the time, screened by the thick fringe of woods.

"The house was really right on the Cape Road, before the woods grew up around it, not in the middle of nowhere," Joey thought.

The plan of going home by way of the Blue Hall Creek was gone with that noise in the clearing. With the possibility of Uncle Tom-Tom hipping and hopping along behind her, Joey chose the quickest, straightest path for home—to the right down the Cape Road, to the right again down the Dog Bone, and back over the ground she had already covered earlier in the morning.

Never was sight so welcome as the white of the house shining through the trees. Having trotted most of the way, Joey was ready to sit down for a while when she finally steamed into the front hall, cool, dark, and oh so safe.

"Is that you, Joey?" Mom's voice from the kitchen mingled with the jam-sweet smell of cooking strawberries.

"Yes, Mom. How long before lunch?"

"Half an hour. Don't forget to wash your hands and face *thoroughly*."

Joey stumped up the stairs and flopped on her bed, kicking off her shoes. The next thing she knew, Mac was pounding on her door, yelling "lunch in five minutes!"

A splashing of cold water and a swipe with a bath towel shouldn't have taken five minutes, but Daddy was already ladling out soup when she reached the table. Donny's black hair was dark with slicked-down dampness, and Mac's red head was equally smooth and shiny. They smiled smugly as Mom cast a critical look at Joey's unstrung pigtails and caked fingernails.

But she only said, "Did you have a nice morning, Joey?"

The twins looked disappointed.

"Pretty good," said Joey, giving them a mean smile. "Daddy, did you know we have a funny clearing right in our own woods?"

"What sort of clearing and where?"

"Mac and I are looking for one!"

"Is it a good place to build a shack?"

The boys and Daddy all spoke at once.

"Between the Dog Bone and the Cape Road, and it's too pretty for one of your old shacks. I found it when I followed the surveyor's line this morning. It's not just a clearing, like the men make when they're cutting trees. It's more like a—well, like a——" She tried to think what the clearing was like, and a word from the *Lady of the Lake*, Daddy's current read-aloud, seemed to suit. "It's a glade," she said triumphantly.

Daddy began to look absent-minded. "I think I know the place you mean. John Rufus took a crew near the Dog Bone to get wood for the corduroy road to the Deer Head Bog last spring."

Joey shook her head so hard that her pigtails smacked her face. She knew the men were always cutting small trees to lay across swampy sections in the roads, like ribs in a piece of corduroy, but no crew of John Rufus's had *ever* planted grass or raised walnut trees. At least not in a clearing in the middle of the woods.

Mom was slicing the cake. "Are you boys thinking of starting another shack this summer?"

"Sure!" Donny looked important. "We've worked out a deal with John Rufus to get all the two-by-fours and boards we need for a week's worth of work on his potato field. After we're finished on the bogs for the day, of course," he added, looking at Daddy.

"What are tubie-fours?" asked Joey.

"Planks that measure two by four inches, dopey."

"This clearing sounds like a neat place for the shack,"

Mac observed, carefully spearing a big piece of frosting
on his fork.

"Oh no!" wailed Joey. "You'd ruin it with your ugly old
shack and then I wouldn't even be allowed to go there,
because you'd have 'no girls allowed' meetings all the
time."

Donny grinned. "I guess that's the place for us, Mac.
Tomorrow's Saturday. We work on the bogs in the morning, start carrying lumber out to the Glade in the afternoon."

"Joey better plan to keep away as of now," Mac said
thoughtfully, "because this will be a secret club house,
and no one but us will ever be allowed in the clearing
again."

"Daddy!" cried Joey. "Tell them they can't build their
shack in my Glade. It isn't fair!"

"I think the boys are only trying to get your goat,
Joey," said Daddy, "but you're right. Two against one
isn't fair. Joey found the Glade, boys, and if she says she
doesn't want a shack in it, then no shack. You've got a
couple of thousand acres to choose from, remember."

The twins didn't seem very downcast, and Joey decided they had been teasing all along.

"Mean things," she muttered to herself.

"I've got to get back to work," Dad said, slipping his
napkin into the ring. "The pickers are coming in three
weeks, and I want to check their shanties this afternoon.
I think some of the shingles blew off them this winter."

"The pickers! In three weeks!"

The traveling gang of workers Daddy hired to pick the
cranberries didn't usually arrive until September.

"There won't be anything to pick!" Donny protested. "Why, the water isn't even off the bogs yet."

"It will be, tomorrow. And I need more than help with picking this year. John Rufus and I have decided to make the swamp at the end of the Deer Head Bog into a new bog. We're going to try out a new variety of berries there. So I've arranged with the Boss to have the gang spend the whole summer with us, instead of going south and following the harvest north."

"How do you make a new bog?" Joey asked curiously. "I thought bogs just were."

"All our bogs were swamps at one time," Daddy said, with a remembering look on his face. "First we have to cut down all the trees and pull out the stumps with a block and tackle. Then we clear out the brush—that's the tough job because it's so slow—dig the ditches for drainage, put a layer of sand over the bottom to make the soil right for growing, and plant the vines. By the time fall comes, we have a new bog."

"No wonder you need a gang to do all that," Donny said, impressed.

"Well, I think it's terrible to have the pickers here for the whole summer!" Joey kicked the rung of her chair. "They make all that noise going in and out past our house, and the kids are all babies or high schoolers. Vangie Smith says the pickers are all wops from Philadelphia."

"Joey," said Daddy, "do you think 'wop' is a pleasant word? Do you enjoy saying it the way you do 'glade'?"

"No," admitted Joey.

"Then my advice is to forget it. Learn three good

words instead. How about 'luminous,' 'fraught,' and 'exquisite'?"

"I know 'exquisite.' "

"Well, then 'humanitarian.' Everybody think of a sentence using all three words by suppertime. Everybody but Mom can use the dictionary. Now I've really got to tear."

"We'd better get back to old Granddaddy Pike," said Mac, giving Donny a punch in the shoulder. "Work tomorrow!"

"It's started to rain," said Joey, giving a satisfied glance out the window. "Ha, ha!"

"Now what are we going to do?" Mac tried to balance his empty glass on his head.

"Whatever you do, you can't do it here. I've got to clean the dining room this afternoon." Beulah marched in with a mop and pail, looking as if she meant business. "Not unless you want to help," she added.

The twins fled to the living room, and Joey trailed glumly after them. The rain might stop the fishing party, but it meant she couldn't do anything outdoors either. She decided to get her sentences ready, and hauled the big dictionary down from the bookcase.

" 'Fraught' means 'loaded,' " she announced. " 'The freight car is fraught with bananas,' I guess." She flipped the pages slowly, wondering if there was anyone in the world who knew all the words. " 'Humanitarian—one who is interested in the welfare of man.' " That was harder. "Donny is not a humanitarian, but Daddy is," she decided finally.

"Luminous" was "giving or emitting light." "Wolf's

eyes are luminous in the dark," Joey said triumphantly. "Now I'm all ready, and you're not."

"Sure we are," Donny said lazily. "You've just given us ours. Dad didn't say we had to get different sentences."

Joey slammed the dictionary shut. She would have liked to throw it at Donny's head.

"It's raining, it's pouring, the old man is snoring. He went to bed, and bumped his head, and couldn't get up in the morning," she chanted tormentingly.

"Shut up!" growled Donny.

"Why does it have to rain during vacation?" groaned Mac.

"To water the plants and fill the rivers," Joey said priggishly.

Donny glared at her. "Dopey! Didn't you hear me say 'shut up'?"

"We're going to be fighting in a minute," observed Mac, "and then Mom will make us all go to our own rooms. We'd better think of something to do first."

"Build a fort on the side porch?"

"We did that last time it rained."

"Play monopoly?"

"We always fight when we play monopoly."

"I know!" Joey jumped off the couch. "Let's go and see John Rufus. He'll be home this afternoon, because he has a little rheumatism when it rains."

"If we take him some fudge he might tell us a story about the old days," said Mac.

"What are we waiting for?" Donny led the stampede into the hall.

"Gosh!" Mac's horrified voice brought them all up short. "Look what Maybelle's done!"

All the wastebaskets in the house had been brought into the hall by Beulah so that she could empty them into one big basket and carry the trash out to the incinerator in one trip. Ten wastebaskets, and all of them were nearly empty. The trash was scattered all over the hall, with Maybelle happily pulling the last few scraps of paper from the study basket.

"She just can't stay away from trash," Donny groaned.

"If she can't find any to play with in the wastebaskets, she takes good papers off the tables and puts them in," Joey added, looking smugly at Wolf.

"How do you know, stupid?" Donny couldn't bear to have anyone say a word against his beloved Maybelle.

"I've seen her," Joey retorted.

"We better get this mess cleaned up before Mom sees it," said Mac. "She wants Maybelle to be sent to the pound like Grandmother wants us to be sent to Philadelphia."

"Mom doesn't really want to get rid of Maybelle," protested Joey. "She couldn't be that mean."

"Well, I'm not taking any chances," said Donny, starting to scoop up the crumpled papers.

They all helped, and before long the hall was neat again, in spite of Maybelle's thinking this was a variation on her favorite game and snatching the papers out of the baskets as soon as they could be put in.

"We'll have to spank her," Donny said reluctantly.

"That's so. She's going to be in real trouble if she doesn't stop doing this."

So Maybelle was hauled up to Mac's room and given a spanking. Joey didn't think it would do much good because Maybelle was too dumb to learn, but she didn't say anything.

And finally they had their slickers on and had set off to John Rufus's house.

"I hope Mom gives me your slicker soon, Mac," Joey said as they squished across the dam. "This one is choking me."

"Grandmother is going to give you a plaid raincoat for your birthday. She thinks girls shouldn't wear boys' clothes. I heard her tell Mom so when Mom asked her to pick up a new slicker for me in Wanamaker's so you could have this one."

Joey moaned. Before long she would be wearing organdy dresses every day.

3

Captain Bones's Treasure

JOHN RUFUS's stove was red hot, on account of the
rheumatism, and he was right next to it, in his big plush
chair. He and Miss Myrtle, his sister who kept house
for him, were listening to a quiz program on the radio.
The three Finches sat down in a row on the couch and
looked at a Sears Roebuck catalog until it was over.
Then Miss Myrtle went off to get cake and milk for
everybody, and John Rufus lit his pipe.

"Mom sent you some homemade fudge." Joey hauled
the limp bag out of her slicker pocket and hung the
coat up again.

"Guess your Ma knows I like her fudge about as well
as anything. Tell her Myrtle wants to send over a pie
next time she does some baking."

Since Mom didn't know anything about the fudge
Joey hoped Miss Myrtle would forget about the pie
before she got around to baking again.

Miss Myrtle came back, and after they all had glasses
of cold milk and huge wedges of chocolate cake Mac
said politely, "John Rufus, we were wondering if you
might feel like telling us a story about the old days."

Suddenly Joey got an idea. "John Rufus," she said

quickly, "do you know anything about that clearing in the woods just north of the Dog Bone?"

John Rufus took his pipe out of his mouth and stared at her.

"How do you know about that clearing, Joanna? Nobody knows where it is but me, and I haven't been there for forty years."

"Forty years!" exclaimed Mac. "A clearing would grow up into woods in forty years."

"Not this clearing. Nothing'll ever change there, except for the inn falling down."

"The inn. Fall down." Mac was getting to sound like a regular echo. "What inn?"

John Rufus looked as if he wished he hadn't said anything. "The Gray Gull," he croaked finally. "That's where the Gray Gull Tavern stood, right in that clearing."

"Oh, John Rufus, you're teasing us. Whoever heard of an inn in the middle of the woods? Who'd stay there?"

"Well now, tadpoles don't always know how wide the river is, do they? Back when my daddy was a boy nobody thought there'd be a railroad. The big road for the stagecoach ran right through these woods on the way from Cape May to Philadelphia. The trip took two days, but everybody wanted to go to Cape May for the summer because of the beach and the sea air."

"And somebody had a hotel along the old Cape Road?"

"A lot of people built taverns along that road. The springs in those stages weren't like no Cadillac shock absorbers, and the more you jolted, the more you wanted places to rest frequent. And the more passengers wanted to rest, the more innkeepers there were to give 'em what they wanted."

"Who built the Gray Gull?" Joey could hardly keep her seat on the couch, she was so excited. To think her clearing had a story like that!

"It was built so long ago I don't reckon anybody knows. In my Grandfather's time, the owner was a man named Edward Dudley."

Mac leaned forward. "John Rufus," he asked, "why did you say the trees will never grow up there?"

John Rufus's eyes half closed as if he were seeing something farther away than the autumn leaves on the wallpaper.

"My grandfather always said that clearing would stay the way it was forever because of the pirate's treasure. Where that's hid the ground stays clear."

"Pirate's treasure!" Even Donny was bouncing up and down on the horsehair prickles now.

"Back before my grandfather or even his grandfather was born, there were pirates along the coast. They liked the inlets fine, the little creeks and the sand bars all ready to snag a navy boat, where no frigate's crew would even try to follow them. And the Cedar River was as good a place as any and better than most.

"Now one of the biggest pirates was Captain Tom Bones, who was specially fond of the Cedar River. He'd come right up and anchor in Holly River Creek. The Gray Gull was a good place to hear the news and wet your whistle, because it was the main stop for the peddlers and the king's messengers and all. And John Dudley, who built the Gray Gull, was a fine honest man,

like many innkeepers, who treated a customer as a customer no matter what color his money was."

"I thought he didn't know who built the Gray Gull,"
whispered Mac.

Joey and Donny kicked him—hard. "Shut up," hissed
Donny.

"But some of the men who came to the inn weren't
so particular about how they talked, and before long
the word got around that Captain Bones was hanging
out in the Gray Gull. One night in May, a whole
squadron of redcoats came after him. They surrounded
the taproom, and he and his crew had to fight for it.
Bones wasn't sure he'd get back to his ship, and he
thought he might as well save the loot he had on him,
brought to pass on to one of the peddlers who smug-
gled such stuff to Philadelphia. And because he trusted
John Dudley, Bones gave him the two things he valued
most—his logbook (with all his prizes listed in it) and
the jeweled peacock. That was a bird made of gold and
rubies and all sorts of fancy stones, a present for a
Spanish princess. Mr. Bones had lifted it right off one
of them big Spanish ships sailing home from Mexico."

"Oh, tell us about the princess!" squealed Joey.

John Rufus's eyes flew wide open. "What princess?"
he asked crossly. "What are you children doing sitting
here? Can't you see the sun's out? Git home!"

4
Alex Appears and Disappears

"How was I supposed to know John Rufus would clam up when I asked him one little question?" Joey swiped at a mosquito with the switch of oak leaves she was holding. "If I hadn't asked the question about the Glade he wouldn't have told us about the pirate's treasure at all. I still don't see why my *second* question shut him up like that."

"Trust a girl to mess things up somehow." Donny swung up on the first rail of the grape arbor and turned his back on her.

Mac always liked to see fair play. "Joey's right," he protested. "Why should her question about the Spanish princess make John Rufus stop telling the story?"

"Because he'd forgotten we were even in the room, stupid, until she had to open her silly mouth. He's old, and he gets in a kind of dream when he remembers things like his grandfather's stories that he heard a long long time ago. And when he realized what he was telling us he stopped."

"But why doesn't John Rufus want us to know about Captain Bones's treasure?" Joey's oak switch took the top right off a tall orange day lily.

Donny shook his head sadly. "How can I be so smart

and have such a dumb brother and sister? Look! You
know as well as I do what the people around here are
like, especially John Rufus. They don't like telling their
tales to outsiders, and we're still outsiders even though
we've lived here all our lives. Besides, they think the
ghosts and bogeymen in the tales will put hants on them
if they talk too much."

"Donny," said Joey breathlessly, "do you know about
Uncle Tom-Tom?"

Mac and Donny exchanged glances. "We've heard of
him," said Donny reluctantly.

"Why didn't you ever tell me about him?"

"Because Dad would have taken the skin off our backs
for scaring a big baby like you."

"Well I know about Uncle Tom-Tom now all right. He
was in the Glade when I was!" Joey announced impressively.

"Did you see him?" Mac's eyes were round with excitement.

"No, but I heard him and so did Wolf. He was hiding
behind a tree and Wolf went after him. I ran all the way
home."

"That settles it! From now on Joey is counted out of
any of our expeditions." Donny banged his fist on the
rail he was sitting on. "She'll be seeing Uncle Tom-Tom
behind every bush and screaming every time a leaf
rustles."

Joey stared at the twins' stubborn faces. How could
they be so mean? But she knew they could, and would,
carry out Donny's threat. And that meant the end of any
fun for her this summer. She couldn't organize her own
expeditions with Uncle Tom-Tom lurking in the woods.

It was time for last-ditch measures. "I'm going to tell Dad."

"If she tells Mom and Dad about hearing Uncle Tom-Tom we might just as well pack our bags for Philadelphia," Mac said gloomily. "Imagine being sent away when we were on the trail of a pirate's treasure!"

"She's got us over a barrel," Donny conceded. "Okay, Joey, we'll make a deal. If you won't tell Dad about hearing Uncle Tom-Tom, we'll take you on some of our fishing trips. But you can't come to the Glade this afternoon when we go to look for Captain Bones's treasure."

Joey didn't like the sound of "some" of the trips, but she could always threaten to tell Dad if the boys didn't take her. And she didn't think she ever wanted to go to the Glade again.

"It's a deal. Where are you going tomorrow? It's your Sunday off, so I know you're planning something."

"Take a lunch and spend the day fishing in the Blue Hall Creek," Mac said.

"Hurray! I haven't been there yet this year."

"You'll have to dig all the worms, of course," Donny said casually.

Joey studied her sneakers. She couldn't push the twins too far. "How many worms will we need?"

"Three cans full, but I suppose you're too big a sissy to dig that many."

"Want to bet? Come on, Wolf!" Joey streaked for the kitchen to get the cans as the twins strode importantly off to work, lunch pails in hand, Maybelle flopping along behind them. But it seemed to be Joey's bad-luck day.

"I'm sorry, Joey." Mom frowned, trying to remember. "Yes, I'm sure Beulah emptied all the trash this morning.

We don't have a single empty can. You'll have to go down to the dump or wait until after lunch."

Joey shuffled out of the kitchen. If she waited until after lunch she'd never have time to fill three cans by tomorrow. But she was scared to go to the dump alone. It was way down in the gloomy woods behind the cornfield, where no one ever went.

"Come on, Wolf," she decided finally. "I'll just have to sing all the way."

"She'll Be Comin' 'Round the Mountain" took Joey through the orchard, past her apple tree, where she and Mac had built a platform for reading and hiding from jungle animals last summer. "Polly Wolly Doodle" lasted right across the cornfield, but her voice sounded pretty thin by the time she got into the shade of those big dark cedar trees.

"I see a buzzard," she told Wolf loudly. The buzzard was coasting in long circles around the giant pine tree way up by Blue Hall Creek. "Kind of looking things over," Joey decided.

"And that thump was only a rabbit taking off. You must have scared him," she added. Wolf hung out his tongue and rolled his eyes at her questioningly. He hadn't smelled any rabbit. "And right down there in that big denty hollow is the trash dump. My, it's dark."

They started cautiously down the edge of the hole, and then Joey caught her foot in an old wheel and rolled the rest of the way. There was a great tinny crash, as what seemed like a million tin cans avalanched down with her, and then she hit—kerplomp!—on a big soft furry thing that didn't move at all.

"Ugh!" she screamed. "Help! I've landed on a dead

monster. Eek! There's something alive here too. Help! Daddy, Mother, Mac, Donny, Wolf, help!" And with the last shriek she managed to get off the dead thing and away from the live thing (which was beginning to clutch) and crawl up the side of the dump.

Wolf was barking ferociously at the top, and getting behind him made Joey feel much safer.

"Turn around and look," Joey told herself, "or you'll never be able to tell what happened. The boys'll never give you another chance if you come back with a story about Uncle Tom-Tom again."

Just thinking that awful name almost scared her into tearing home, but she grabbed the scruff of Wolf's neck and stuck her head over the edge of the incline.

"Great jumping jehoshaphat!"

There, right below her, at the end of a slide of knocked-off sand and tin cans, was her "monster," a huge plush wing chair. And crouched in it was the "wild animal"—the skinniest boy Joey had ever seen.

"Wow, you sure scared me!" she called. "What are you doing down in our trash dump?"

The boy closed his eyes and shook like the baby rabbit Maybelle had brought home in her mouth one day. Joey began to feel sorry for him. He had gotten a bigger fright than she had, she guessed.

"Are you new in Cedarville?" she asked and then thought that was a silly question, because no Cedarviller would turn up in the Holly River trash dump. They never ventured an inch away from their own main street and truck gardens. Not even new ones, and, anyway, no one was ever new in Cedarville. "Come on up."

The boy twisted himself out of the chair and began to

crawl slowly up the side of the dump. He seemed to like being given something definite to do. Joey waited until he was almost at the top, and then gave him a good helping pull up beside her by grabbing one of his overall straps.

Close to, he looked even more like the rabbit, she decided. He had the same round brown eyes and very short tan hair. "And quivery nose." Joey chuckled to herself. "But he's awfully bony."

The boy showed no signs of wanting to run away, so she let go of him and asked briskly, "What's your name?"

"Alex Wriggly-Witch," he muttered, his nose quivering harder than ever.

Joey stared. This certainly was a funny boy. Who had ever heard of a name like that? And he had a strange way of saying it, like coughing. He tried to slip sideways, but she grabbed hold of that handy overall strap.

"Where are you going?"

"It is time I eat."

"Oh, come home for lunch with me. Mom won't mind. She always has plenty of food."

"No. I must go home."

"Well, home can't be very near. The closest houses are in Cedarville, and that's six miles. You'll be hollow down to the soles of your feet by the time you get there. Come on!"

And he came, with a lot of feet shuffling and nose quiverings, though.

Mom nearly dropped the potato salad when she saw a perfectly strange boy dragged in the door. "Now where did you find him?" she asked Joey.

"In the trash dump. I think he needs a good lunch," she added in a whisper. "His name is Alex Wriggly-Witch."

"Joey," said Mom grimly, "I think you've been sitting in the sun too long. Boys don't grow in trash dumps, and even if they did, they wouldn't have names like Alex Wriggly-Witch."

"My name," squeaked Alex suddenly, "is . . ." and he coughed it out again.

"Of course," said Mom. "Rig-*lay*-witz!"

"How do you spell it?" Joey wanted to know. "It sure sounded like Wriggly-Witch to me."

Alex looked at Mom helplessly, and she handed him her "Things To Do" pad and the pencil she tried to remember to keep beside it.

"R-y-g-l-e-w-i-c-z!" Joey spelled it out over Alex's

shoulder. "Zowee! How do you remember those letters?"

"How do you remember how to spell your name?" Alex retorted with unexpected spirit.

"Why, you must come from one of the families that have taken farms on the state land just south of Holly River," Mom said.

Alex nearly smiled and his nose stopped quivering.

"Then you must be a Po—— You must be Polish!" Joey said, in surprise.

Alex nodded. He seemed to have lost his sudden flash of spirit.

"Well, show Alex where he can wash his hands. Lunch is practically on the table."

Joey escorted him to the pantry sink and stood by with the hand towel Mom kept there. Alex stood in front of the sink without moving.

"Where is the pump?" he asked finally.

Joey wanted to call to Mom to share this joke of a boy who didn't know how faucets worked, but she stopped herself just in time. She didn't want that nose to start quivering again.

"Here." She turned on the hot water and washed her own hands carefully. "Now it's your turn."

Alex stuck his hands gingerly under the water, and an honest-to-goodness smile spread across his face.

"Ah!" he sighed happily. He rubbed the soap round and round, working up a big lather.

Joey grinned and flicked some of the water from her wet hands into his face. Quick as a wink Alex reached out and planted a big lump of suds on the end of her nose.

"No fights," called Mom from the doorway. "Luncheon is served, ladies and gentlemen."

Joey was horrified at the way Alex ate. He kept his knife in his right hand and with it troweled gobs of potato salad around the pieces of wiener he speared firmly on his fork. The size of the pile he could tuck in his mouth at one time was breath-taking. It was so big that he couldn't get his mouth closed again. It was a good thing the twins had taken sandwiches with them, because they liked heckling bad manners.

Luckily, Mom didn't seem to notice. She kept passing Alex food, and Joey counted that he had three wieners, two big helpings of potato salad, two pieces of cake, and three glasses of milk, not to mention pickles and sliced tomatoes which she couldn't keep track of.

"I bet you'll be sick," she whispered as they left the table.

"It is worth it," Alex said with a sigh.

Joey nodded. She could understand that feeling.

"Why don't you spend the afternoon?" she suggested. "We could go fishing."

"No. My mother will be needing me. But I will come again soon." He turned to Mom shyly. "Thank you for the good meal." He gave a little bow, and as he bent over something tumbled out of his overalls pocket with a clink. With a darting movement he had scooped it up almost before it hit the floor, but Joey saw what it was. A battered old tin cup. So he had been hunting for old dishes and things in the dump.

Before she or Mom could say anything Alex was gone.

5

Footprints in the Sand

MAC and Donny were so full of their first half-day of work that they forgot to mention their trip to the Glade until after supper.

The family had settled down on the screened-in porch —the twins and Joey on the glider, Mom in a rocking chair, and Daddy stretched out in his lounge chair under the floor lamp. Daddy opened the *Lady of the Lake* and started to read. Suddenly Joey remembered.

"Did you go to the Glade?" she whispered to Mac.

Daddy frowned and stopped. "Did you ask a question, Joanna?"

Joey gulped. "Yes, Daddy. I asked Mac if he and Donny had gone to the Glade to look for Captain Tom Bones's peacock and logbook. The *Lady of the Lake* made me think of the Glade."

Mom put down the sweater she was knitting.

"Whatever are you talking about, Joey? Who is Captain Tom Bones, and why should he hide a book and peacock in a clearing in our woods?"

"He was a pirate, Mom!" Mac's eyes sparkled in the lamplight. "John Rufus told us about him yesterday. Joey asked John Rufus if he had ever seen the Glade, and he remembered this pirate story his grandfather had told him."

"There was an inn in the Glade," Joey said, "the Gray Gull Inn, and when the redcoats captured Tom Bones he left his jeweled peacock (that was a present for a *princess* only he stole it) and his logbook with the owner of the inn, John Dudley."

"What makes you think they're still there?" Daddy had forgotten all about the *Lady of the Lake* and Joey's rude interruption.

"Because the clearing that has pirate treasure hidden in it will never grow up until the treasure is dug up," Donny said impressively.

"And John Dudley must have kept the things, because Captain Bones said he would come back and claim them and he never did."

"What happened to Bones?" asked Mom.

"John Rufus didn't say—at least he was going to and then Dopey here had to mess everything up by asking a question about some old princess." Donny snorted.

"A princess! Say, John Rufus has been telling you quite a story. Who was the princess?"

"That's what I was trying to find out," Joey explained. "John Rufus said Captain Bones had taken the golden peacock off a Spanish ship sailing to Spain from Mexico. It was a gift for the Spanish princess. Who would she be, Daddy?"

Daddy hauled himself off the lounge chair. "I can't tell you who she was, but I think I can show you what a Spanish princess in the days of piracy looked like."

"You were lucky to have John Rufus tell you all this,"

said Mom. "He won't usually talk about the old days of the county, even to Dad."

"We'll probably be able to get him to tell more about Tom Bones and the Gray Gull," boasted Joey, "now that we've got him started."

"I hope so. This is like starting an exciting book and then losing it before you get to the end," Mac complained.

"Here we are." Daddy came back on the porch with a big, flat book in his hands. He held it under the lamp and turned the pages carefully. "Take a look at your princess, Joey. The Infanta Margarita Teresa and her ladies-in-waiting."

The twins and Joey crowded in to look. The picture in the book showed a little girl with a funny lot of wavy blond hair and calm blue eyes standing in the middle of a shadowy room. All around her were ladies in rich gowns.

"She was a Spanish princess," said Daddy, "and the man at the easel is the artist who painted the picture. His name was Velasquez, and he must have had a sense of humor to paint himself painting the picture."

"Look at that great stiff long dress she's wearing," Joey said. "And I complain about organdy's scratching. I don't see how she could walk."

"A gold peacock would fit right into that room, wouldn't it?" remarked Mac. "I bet the captain of that Spanish ship was hopping mad when Tom Bones took his treasure."

"He probably didn't live to be mad very long," Donny said darkly.

"If the peacock came from Mexico, the Spanish cap-

tain had probably stolen it in the first place from the poor
Aztec Indian who made it, so he very likely deserved
what he got." Daddy shut the book.

"This conversation is getting very bloodthirsty," protested Mom. "Let's get back to poor Ellen."

So Daddy picked up the *Lady of the Lake* again, and
in two minutes Spanish treasure and wicked pirates were
replaced by the fiery cross and loyal clansmen.

"Don't forget that I'm going fishing with you tomorrow," Joey said to Donny and Mac as they climbed
sleepily up the stairs. "I filled three cans with worms,
and it took me all afternoon. I had to make another trip
to the trash dump for cans after that Alex left."

"Okay," yawned Mac. "You spent the afternoon better
than we did. We didn't find a thing in that Glade of
yours except about fifty million mosquitoes. You were
right about the bricks being there," he added generously.

"We found one other thing," Donny said softly. "There
was a patch of sand near that sumac tree, the one you
thought Uncle Tom-Tom was behind. And what do you
think we saw in the sand?"

Joey held her breath.

"Two footprints!"

It seemed to Joey that she dreamed about Uncle Tom-
Tom all night long. He chased her through the woods
and swamps and over the bogs waving a golden bird that
had one red eye and cried out in a voice like Vangie
Smith's, "He'll get you for sure for saying that. He'll put
a hant on you for sure." And just as the bird's beak
reached her flying hair Vangie's voice changed into
Mac's, shouting, "Everybody that plans to go fishing
better get up," and she woke up and was safe.

Right after breakfast Mom packed three big paper bags full of lunch and filled a thermos bottle with lemonade. Donny loaded all the supplies, including the cans of worms, into his knapsack, and they all took turns carrying it.

They walked down the Dog Bone, cool and silent in the early morning, past the gravel pit and the surveyor's path, to the Cape Road, where they turned left. The Cape Road was wide and mossy, ideally suited for silent Indian walks.

"Let's play Lenni-Lenape," suggested Joey. "I'm Princess Snow Flower."

"Me Big King Nummy," grunted Donny.

"Me Squanto, friend of white man." Mac raised his right hand. "Me stalk deer."

By the time the deer had been killed, with a great deal of noisy help in the hunting from Wolf and Maybelle, they had reached the place where the Blue Hall Creek flowed across the Cape Road. Donny signaled a turn, and they swung left along its bank.

"Here's the place," Mac said finally.

"And here's John Rufus!" Joey exclaimed.

Sure enough, there he was, sitting on a log, with his back against a big pine tree, his fish line trailing lazily in the brown creek.

"How're they biting, John Rufus?" asked Joey.

"So-so."

The three Finches silently got out their own lines and cut themselves poles from likely saplings. Mac and Donny had regular fishhooks, but Joey had to use a bent pin to hold her worm. She dropped her line in the water and made herself comfortable on the other end of John

Rufus's log. The twins had gone upstream to try their luck.

It was very quiet. The mosquitoes buzzed more loudly as the day got hotter, and a woodpecker rat-tat-tatted in a nearby tree, but there were no other sounds in the sleepy woods. Sometimes a frog's head would poke out of the water at the mossy edge of the stream. Joey wanted to giggle at the way the round popeyes stared at her, but she knew better than to make a sound.

"Ah!" said John Rufus suddenly.

His line had begun to jerk violently. He started to pull it in gently, pausing between pulls to make sure that the jerks were still going on at the other end.

"Must be a big one," breathed Joey.

He got the baited end of the line right to the bank,

and, bending over, gave the line a sharp tug. There was a little whiskered catfish spinning in mid-air.

"It's just a baby," Joey said in disappointment.

John Rufus took the hook out gently and tossed the fish back.

That was their only bite of the morning. When the sun was straight over the trees the twins joined Joey and John Rufus for lunch. Their luck had been no better.

"Too dry today," said John Rufus.

After they had eaten their sandwiches there was a piece of Miss Myrtle's chocolate cake all around.

"Myrtle kinda thought I might see you today," John Rufus remarked.

Joey stretched out comfortably on soft pine needles and squinted at the sky. "Not a cloud in sight. We can stay here all afternoon if we want to."

There was a drowsy silence. John Rufus leaned back and closed his eyes.

"John Rufus," Mac said softly, "what happened to Captain Bones when the redcoats surrounded him in the taproom of the Gray Gull?"

"Why, he got clean away. He and his crew were good fighters and they were cornered, so they fought twice as good. They cut their way through those soldiers like you'd cut a piece of cheese. Once they'd gotten to the ship there was no holding them. They sailed down the Cedar River and slipped off to another hide-out."

"Did Bones ever come back for his treasure?" Joey's voice was hardly louder than the hum of a mosquito.

"Nope. Tom Bones and his men were captured in fair fight aboard their own ship a year later and hanged in

Charleston, down in Carolina. He never saw the Gray
Gull again."

"Then the treasure was John Dudley's, wasn't it?"

"No sirree. The Dudleys felt it was still just something
they had to look after. The idea being that if any of
Bones's descendants ever came to claim it the Dudleys
would turn the bird and the book over to them."

"And did anyone come to claim it?"

"Not so far as I know of. But there was talk in my
grandfather's time of the captain coming to look after
the peacock himself."

A big cold shiver whipped down Joey's backbone.
"You mean his ghost comes back—to the Glade?"

"That's what they say." John Rufus nodded.

6
A New Girl

FOR the next three weeks Joey kept hoping that she would see Alex again, but he never turned up. She guessed he was too busy helping his family settle into their new home or else he was ashamed of her seeing that tin cup and knowing he was so poor that he had to get dishes out of other people's trash dumps.

She did wish she could find someone to play with. Mac and Donny had started to work in earnest on the bogs. They had to be on the job by seven and they didn't finish until four, when they grabbed their poles and high-tailed it for the creek. Joey was allowed to go fishing with them only once under the new agreement.

If it was hot they skinned into their trunks and went for the swimming hole after work. Joey tried tagging along, but Donny had a way of diving under the black water and pinching her toes like a snapping turtle, so she soon decided to take her swim earlier in the afternoon—alone!

On Saturday afternoons and Sundays the boys had to pick the bugs off John Rufus's potatoes (in order to earn their precious lumber), and any spare time was spent tramping the woods in search of a shack site. But they couldn't find a place that suited them, and Joey was stubborn about not letting them build it in the Glade.

She ached to find out more about the treasure Captain Tom Bones had left at the Gray Gull. The twins said loftily that they had better things to think about, which meant they were more interested in fishing at the moment. John Rufus, her only hope, seemed to be sorry he had ever told the story in the first place and shut up like a frozen clam when she tried to ask him about it. And she was afraid to go treasure hunting in the Glade by herself because of Uncle Tom-Tom and his evil eye.

So when Mom called one morning, "Joey, the pickers are driving over the dam," she practically jumped with joy, because at last something was happening.

Rattle, clank, bump. With a lot of horn-blowing and happy shouting, the rattletrap cavalcade drew up at the front door. Three model-T trucks were loaded with what looked like mattresses and orange crates, with a wicker baby carriage bouncing on top of one load. Five dirty old sedans, flying foxtails and pennants, were stuffed with people, jabbering at the top of their voices. Joey put her hands over her ears.

An enormous man with crinkly gray hair, who looked a little like the picture of Christopher Columbus in the fourth grade history book, heaved himself out of the first car and marched up to the front door.

Mom pulled Joey away from the living-room window.

"Come on," she said. "That's the Doge. I want you to meet him. This is his first trip to Holly River. Dad always made the arrangements for the Doge to send down a gang of pickers up in Philadelphia and John Rufus supervised them when they got here. But this year, the Doge decided to come down in person."

The Doge beamed when they opened the front door, and shook hands with Mom.

"I'm real glad to see you again, Mrs. Finch," he boomed.

"This is my daughter Joanna, Mr. De Sipio. Joey, here at last is the Doge."

Mr. De Sipio gave a booming laugh. "So Mr. Finch still calls me *Il Doge*. I must say that's a pretty nice compliment. And I suppose we're going to live in Little Venice again?"

"You're absolutely right. Just drive right up there and settle in. Mr. Finch will come up this afternoon about four to see that everything is all right and make the arrangements for the crew to start working."

"Mom, what does he mean by calling the shanties Little Venice?" hissed Joey. "And why do you and Daddy call him the Doge?"

"Ask Mr. De Sipio," smiled Mom.

"In Italy, girlie," explained Mr. De Sipio, "there's a city called Venice, that's surrounded by water. The ruler of Venice was a man called the duke or *Il Doge*. Your daddy went to Venice once, and because we're Italian-Americans and the shanties are surrounded by water, he calls me the Doge and them Little Venice. His idea of a joke, see?"

Joey didn't quite see, but she flapped her pigtails as if she did because she didn't want to hurt the Doge's feelings.

"Why don't you ride up to Little Venice with me now? The little Lorenzo kid is just about your age, and she could show you what a good system we've worked out for settling into a new place."

"Go ahead, Joey," said Mom. "It'll be a good experience."

When Mom and Dad said that it usually meant, you won't like this but we want you to do it anyway and someday you'll be glad you did. So Joey walked reluctantly down the front walk with the Doge and climbed into his rattly old car.

They skittered up the sandy road, past the packing house, the barrel house, over a small dam that didn't have a name, and there they were. The shanties were crude wooden houses scattered around a clearing in an angle between the end of the Brook Bog and the side of another smaller bog. There was swamp on the other two sides, which was why Daddy said the shanties were surrounded by water. The one two-storied shantie was "the Doge's Palace." Here Mr. De Sipio pulled up.

"All out," he shouted, and his fat wife and four tall sons tumbled out of the car and began to pull wicker baskets of food and dishes down from the first truck. Joey stood by the car, feeling silly with nothing to do and no one to talk to. Suddenly the Doge roared, "Hey there! Baptista Lorenzo! Come over here!"

A dark-haired girl about Joey's size wiggled out of the busy group around the truck and walked slowly over to the car.

"This is Joanna Finch, the boss's daughter. You want to take good care of her. Show her how we do things." He pulled one of Joey's pigtails, twitched one of Baptista's long curls, and strode away.

Baptista's soft round eyes stared at Joey for a minute. Joey stared right back. She couldn't think of anything to say.

"Come meet my father and mother," Baptista said finally. Joey couldn't help but admire her voice. It was sort of like the sound of the Japanese bells Grandmother had hanging up in her front hall.

"Okay," she said. "Where are they?"

Baptista led the way to the shack on the edge of the Brook Bog. A very plump lady and a very small wiry man were shouting directions as two big boys carried in an iron bed head. As Baptista came up they all stopped what they were doing and smiled at her.

"Mama, Pop," she said softly, "this is Joanna the owner's daughter. Joanna, these are my parents, and over there are Tony and Frank, my brothers."

"Well," said Pop, "what did I tell you? Yesterday Baptista was complaining about leaving all her pals in Philadelphia, and today she already has a new friend."

All the Lorenzos beamed at Joey.

Baptista giggled. "And here comes our little Carmencita." A very pretty girl, with dark curly hair like Baptista's, came toward them, pushing the wicker carriage Joey had noticed on top of a truck. And in it, surrounded by pots and pans, sat the fattest baby Joey had ever seen. Her eyes were nothing but creases in her red cheeks, and her waving hands were like fat little starfish.

"That is Bianca, my other sister, pushing Carmencita," explained Baptista.

"Baptista," said Mrs. Lorenzo, "there is nothing for you to do here this afternoon. Carmencita will take her nap right in the carriage, and the rest of us will be busy putting things away. You go and play with Joanna. Supper will be at six."

"But Mr. De Sipio said I was to see how you settled in," protested Joey.

"Look at the trucks," Baptista said simply.

They were already bare. The last few odds and ends were being tossed down into waiting hands by the men who had unloaded them in such a short time.

"That is what he meant," explained Pop. "We have loaded and unloaded our things so many times that we can do it in a few minutes, with everybody helping everybody else."

Joey felt disappointed, but she liked the idea of having somebody to play with.

"Come on down to my house," she said to Baptista.

"Run along," nodded Mrs. Lorenzo.

"Do you travel around all the time?" Joey asked enviously as they walked over the dam.

Baptista looked horrified. "No indeed," she said. "In the winter we live in Philadelphia. All the pickers who work for Mr. De Sipio do. Pop works in a shoe factory and all of us go to school."

She looked curiously out over the long, flat tangle of green vines that were the bog, at the thick trees beyond. "It's awful lonely here, isn't it?"

"Haven't you been on bogs before?" asked Joey. She knew they were all pretty much like Holly River.

"No. Our family has gone to Hammonton to pick peaches every summer till now. Pop wanted to go here, because it meant the whole summer in one place."

Joey couldn't understand how anyone could help but like the bogs right off the bat. Especially anyone doomed to spend her winters in Philadelphia. She decided to change the subject before she got to worrying about living with Grandmother again.

"Do you like to read?" she asked.

"Oh, I love to! I get a book every week from the library."

"Can you go to the library every single week?"

"Why sure. It's only five blocks away. All the kids go on Saturday morning."

"Gosh!" Joey sighed with envy. "We have to wait for the book truck from the County library to come to school before we get any new books, and by the time it gets around to us again, I've read all the books about three times. And the worst of it is the way some kids request the same old book over and over. I bet I've read *The Japanese Twins* thirty-five times, just because Vangie Smith asks to have it renewed every single visit."

"Alma, my best friend in Philadelphia, is just like that. She holds everybody up, looking at all the new books that have come in, and in the end she chooses *The Little Colonel*. She's worn one copy right out, and the librarian had to order a new one. I get so mad at her!"

They dwelt companionably on the twin shortcomings of Alma and Vangie in silence for a while.

"Here we are," said Joey, leading the way into the front hall.

"Joey!" yelled Mom from the back of the house. "Hurry and help me with the clothes. It's starting to pour."

Sure enough as they tore out the back door a rapidly increasing sheet of water met them. Mom, her hair already like Maybelle's when she had been in the swimming hole, was wildly snatching armfuls of sheets and shirts off the line and pitching clothespins in the big basket. Joey and Baptista started in at the other end, where Beulah had draped the smaller things.

"Whew!" gasped Mom, when they finally staggered through the back door, three around the heavy basket. She held up a dripping shirt. "Exactly right for ironing," she said proudly. "We made it in time."

Joey and Baptista had to laugh at that.

Mom rocked back on her heels and looked at Baptista. "Now where did *you* come from?" she asked.

"From Philadelphia," Baptista said politely.

"This is Baptista Lorenzo, Mom," Joey said hastily. "She's with the pickers."

Mom beamed. "That means you'll have a girl to play with this summer."

Joey looked at Baptista significantly. All parents were the same when you came right down to it.

"Mom," she said, "after we've helped you hang up the clothes in the cellar, may we play dress-up in the attic?"

Mom peered at the window. Rain was sluicing over it like a gray curtain. "As long as this keeps up, you may," she decided.

"I've never been in an attic before," confided Baptista as they clambered up the narrow little stairs a while later.

"Every house has to have an attic," Joey said scornfully.

"Not apartments, and that's where everybody I know lives," said Baptista, just as scornfully.

Then she quit talking, overcome at the paradise that met her eyes at the head of the stairs.

Every toy the Finches had ever had was still there, waiting to be wanted again. Mom made them go on the

rotation system, a certain number of playthings in their
rooms, the rest stored up here until they wanted to trade.
Rows of dolls sat grandly on top of Grandmother's old
red velvet settee. A whole fleet of trucks, an entire navy
of toy ships lay over a box of electric train tracks. Blocks
and games, a gigantic, grinning rocking horse, a battered
marionette theater announcing Jack and the Beanstalk—
the treasures were endless.

Joey hardly gave them a second glance. Most of them
had been put up here too recently to be exciting yet.
She headed straight for the big trunks under the eaves.

"Come pick yourself a costume," she invited, throwing the biggest and oldest one open.

No one answered. Baptista was staring awe-struck at
the dolls.

"Are all these yours?" she asked in a whisper.

Joey could hardly hear her above the rain on the roof.
"Sure," she said. "They're old ones. Come decide what
you want to be."

"Be?" Baptista stared at her just as blankly as she'd
stared at the dolls. "What do you mean?"

"What character you want to be. In our story. Or
would you rather choose a story first and then decide?
We usually do it this way because we know who we
want to be and then make up a story."

Baptista came over and looked at the red-hooded cape
on top of the other things in the trunk, as if it might
give her a clue.

"Like playing tea party? Or going to the store?"

"Well, sort of. Only we usually act out a story from
the Bible or a book, or make one up about cowboys and
Indians and stuff. We dress up in these costumes." Joey

found it hard to explain, and Baptista's eyes looked bigger and blanker than ever.

"Joey!" Mac's voice echoed up the stairs. "Do you want to play stagecoach? Mom said you were up here."

His head appeared through the railing around the stair well.

"Another girl!" he snorted.

Joey expected Baptista would get mad, but she smiled prettily.

"I hope you don't mind my being here," she said sweetly.

Mac blushed. "Gosh no," he said quickly. "And neither does Donny." A red head appeared beside his, grimacing as if its owner had been kicked. "What do you want to play?"

"Why don't you choose?" suggested Baptista.

Both faces grinned and vanished, to reappear in a second at the top of the stairs.

"This is Baptista," said Joey. "And these are my brothers, Mac and Donny."

The twins actually gave a sort of bow. "How would you like to play highway robbers and stagecoach on the old Cape Road?" asked Mac. "Joey, you could be the driver and Baptista could be the passenger, and Donny could be the robber, and I could be the sheriff."

"They didn't have sheriffs then," said Joey. She didn't think being the driver sounded like much fun.

"Well, a soldier then. I could still have a fight with the highway robber."

"Hunkers on the cape!" Joey yelled quickly.

"The soldier should have that," Mac yelled back.

"Joey asked first," said Donny loudly, waving toward

Baptista in a way that meant "don't fight in front of outsiders."

Mac finally took Uncle Tony's uniform jacket from the war. Donny put on the regular villain's outfit—Daddy's old tail coat—and Baptista got in the swing of things and rooted out a pink bonnet and a heavy blue silk dress that actually had a hoop under the skirt. With her long curls she looked like a real old-fashioned lady.

She squealed with excitement when Joey put on the red cape. "That's exactly like one I saw when our class went to the museum last winter. The lady took it out of the case to show us the secret pocket. Does that have one?"

"No," said Joey reluctantly, "at least not that I know of."

"Where was it on the cape you saw?" asked Mac eagerly.

"Not on—in!" giggled Baptista. "It was sort of sewed in one of the seams. Here, I'll show you."

She took the cape and ran careful fingers down the seam on the left side. "Right about he——" Two of the fingers vanished and she let out another squeal. "Here! There is one in this cape. With a piece of paper in it!"

Joey could hardly contain herself. "Pull it out!" she howled. "Let us see it."

The paper was yellow-brown and very ragged. The writing was brown too, and so spidery that they could hardly make it out.

> GRAY GULL HOSTELRY
> *1 qt. Jamaica Rum, 44 cents*
> *1 qt. cherry, 14 cents*

"It looks like a bill," said Donny finally.

"There's something on the other side too," said Joey, dancing with excitement.

Baptista turned the paper over. The script was different, rounder and not as elegant, and rather scrawled, as if the writer had been in a hurry.

> I have undertaken to set a certain guest
> on his way to D. B. remember the Navy
> Of Tarshish key beneath door stone.
>   *Yr. affec. Daughter*

7

The Ghost of Captain Bones

"IT IS so a clue!" Joey glared at Donny across the breakfast table. The old bill was lying peacefully by the maple-syrup jug, not looking like the beginning of a fight. "Isn't it, Daddy? Like in that Sherlock Holmes story you read last night."

Mom looked at Dad accusingly. "I thought you were going to start *David Copperfield* last night. So that's what happens when I decide to be conscientious and spend an evening in the sewing room."

Mom hated sewing, and the only way she could make herself do it was to shut herself in her sewing room on the third floor where she wouldn't be distracted into doing something that was more fun.

What Mom called his "guilty smile" crept across Dad's face. "I was," he said, "but Mac asked me what a clue was, and I got side-tracked."

"Yes, and a clue is like the note on the back of that old bill," said Joey triumphantly. "It's a hint. Only nobody can figure out what it's hinting," she added dolefully.

"I think it shows that there was really an old inn called the Gray Gull, like John Rufus said," Mac con-

tributed unexpectedly, "and I think we ought to go to
the Glade and investigate some more."

"Not on Sunday!" It was Donny's turn to glare. "We
were going to start our shack."

"You can build it in the Glade," Joey put in hastily.

"I thought you said the Glade was too pretty for a
shack," said Daddy teasingly.

"Well, maybe Mac and Donny will build a pretty
shack this time," said Joey, not very hopefully. "But,
gosh, Sunday seems like a long time to wait. Why, this
is only Monday."

"The time will go quickly," promised Mom, "now
that you have Baptista to play with."

She was partly right. Joey and Baptista found plenty
to do and the days seemed to fly by, but Joey was in
such a fever of impatience to get to the Glade that time
couldn't fly fast enough to suit her. And then it was
Sunday morning at last, and the Finches were finishing
breakfast.

"Do you think we should take the bill of sale with
us to the Glade?" Joey wanted to know. "The note on
the back of it is the important clue."

"How can an old note help us locate Captain Bones's
peacock, when we don't even understand what the note's
about?" Donny retorted.

"We probably won't have time to look for the treasure,
anyway," Mac added. "We're going to be too busy working on the shack."

"Where did you put the bill of sale?" Dad asked
casually.

"In my atlas," Joey answered, before she turned on
the boys indignantly. "If you think I'm going to let you

build your shack in my Glade, unless you help me look
for the treasure, why——"

"Someone's knocking on the back screen," Mom
interrupted diplomatically. "Joey, please run and see
who it is."

It was Baptista.

"Come over to my house and play paper dolls," she
said. "Mama gave me the last Sears Roebuck catalog,
and I'll go halfsy on the toys and furniture."

"Paper dolls! We're going to the Glade to see if we
can learn more about the old inn."

Baptista's eyes turned pink, and Joey felt mean.

"You can come too," she said quickly. "The boys will
be glad to have you, and with two of us they won't
pick on me so much. Come on!"

"But I have Carmencita. I've got to look after her
all day."

Sure enough, there by the back steps was the wicker-
basket carriage, minus pots and pans, with Carmencita
looking for all the world like a fat teddy bear.

"Bring her along," said Joey. "There's a clear trail
almost all the way for the carriage, and we can watch
her in the Glade as well as at home."

"All right." Baptista began to twinkle again.

Mac and Donny were flatteringly cheerful when Joey
announced that Baptista was coming along. They even
accepted Carmencita.

"We can put provisions in her carriage," Mac said.

"Is it all right if we spend the whole day in the Glade,
Mom?" asked Joey.

Mom tickled Carmencita under the chin. "Sure," she

said, "you can stay there as long as you like. Stay all
night!"

"Can we, Mom?"

"Can we camp out?"

"All of us?"

The thought of really camping out, sleeping like King
Nummy and his Lenni-Lenape braves around the embers
of a carefully built watch fire, gave Joey bubbles and
butterflies under her belt.

"What have I said now?" Mom asked Carmencita,
who giggled sympathetically. "Actually, I was only
being funny. I don't want you to camp out, especially
so far from the house."

The three Finches set up a yell of protest. Even
Maybelle and Wolf began to howl.

"You just said we could!" protested Joey.

"No, I—well, maybe—no I—oh, go ask your father.
If he says 'yes,' it's all right with me."

The noise of three running pairs of feet was terrific.

Poor Daddy, who had his desk piled high with
accounting books, looked as if the thundering herd had
ridden right over him.

"Help!" he said finally, after everybody had tried to
speak at once for about five minutes. "King Nummy
would like permission to build a shack in the Glade for
Wolf and Maybelle to spend the night in? Is that right?"

The boys and Joey couldn't help laughing. Dad
appointed Donny to explain what they wanted.

"I see that there are two sides to this question," he
said, when Donny had finished. Everybody groaned.

"But all things considered, I don't see any reason

why you can't spend the night in the Glade." Everybody cheered.

"Provided," and Dad frowned as if he were trying to look like the picture of Grandmother on the wall, "you follow a few rules to the letter." Everybody groaned again.

"No fire unless you have two buckets of water or a fire extinguisher. At least one layer of pine branches and two blankets between you and the ground. And the first one to start a fight has to come home. I suppose I don't need to tell you to take Wolf and Maybelle," he added.

"How about Baptista and Carmencita?" asked Joey.

"Mrs. Lorenzo will have to decide about that. I personally have my doubts about Carmencita's qualifying as Indian scout material, but we'll see."

"She could be a papoose," suggested Joey.

While the twins loaded their precious supply of nails, tools, and two-by-fours into Donny's big red freight wagon, Baptista pushed Carmencita home at a dead run. She came back with the sad report that both of them would have to be back at Little Venice by suppertime.

"Still, you'll have the whole day," Joey said comfortingly. "Let's go get the blankets from Mom."

Mom had her head in the blanket closet. "Will four blankets apiece be enough?" she asked in a funny echoing voice. "At this time of year, you shouldn't get cold at night."

"Gosh yes!" Joey scooped up the first load, five blankets Uncle Tony had brought back from the army. "These are neat."

Baptista staggered out with another load, and they went back for one more.

"Food next," said Donny. He had made out a list from his Scout handbook and was checking things off on it.

Mom contributed wieners, rolls, tomatoes, oranges, half a chocolate cake, a dozen ham sandwiches, and a bowl of potato salad. "This isn't very woodsman-like," she apologized, "but it's all I have on hand."

Joey thought privately that cake and salad were a lot better than baked beans and raw potatoes, though she didn't say so, of course.

"How about a jug of lemonade?" she asked.

"Coming up," said Mom.

"Can we borrow the fire extinguisher in the upstairs hall?" asked Mac.

"As long as you bring it back. And better each one take your ponchos and a box of matches and don't forget your flashlights."

"How about pajamas?"

Joey wished she hadn't said anything when the boys wheeled on her scornfully. "Pajamas! Why don't you put your bed on the wagon and take that along? Girls!"

"My, you boys know all about camping," Baptista said admiringly. "You must have been doing it a long time."

Mac and Donny started on a story of their camping adventures at scout camp, and Joey's error was forgotten.

Finally they were ready. Baptista and Joey had a firm hold on the handle of Carmencita's heaped carriage, and the twins stood at each end of their wagon.

"All set," said Donny giving a last check to his list. "No, wait! We forgot kindling. Joey, you run back to the woodshed and get some. We'll start ahead slowly."

Joey started to argue, but Baptista gave her a poke with her elbow.

"Go ahead," she whispered. "He just wants to make you mad."

Joey smiled as sweetly as Baptista and called, "Okay, you go ahead."

Donny looked disappointed.

The woodshed was a little black cave built on the back of the garage. It had a soft dirt floor, and great shadowy tiers of logs lined the walls. The kindling was in a cranberry packing box away in the back. Joey ran right up to the door and rushed in, because she didn't want to miss any of the fun of the expedition. But she ran out faster than she had run in.

"Something awful's in the woodshed," she screamed. "It's got eyes, and I think it's Uncle Tom-Tom. Eee!"

If she hadn't been so scared, Joey would have laughed at the way people came tumbling from all directions, like the clowns in the circus over at Atlantic City. Mom from the back porch, Dad from the study, the twins up the driveway, and last of all, Baptista, at a bumpy trot, with Carmencita's carriage careening at her heels. Even John Rufus came hobbling down the road, taking great care to keep the dust from getting on his Sunday suit.

Mac got to the woodshed door a good length before any of the others, and he dashed right in. He certainly didn't seem to be afraid of Uncle Tom-Tom or anything else being in there. Joey heard a rattle of kindling and a sort of scurrying sound, as if an animal was trying to run out of the shed, and then Mac yelled, "Got him!"

Joey screamed again and hid her face (shamefully)

against Mom's waist. Donny and Dad had reached the
scene of the fray by this time, and they helped Mac
drag out his captive.

"Good gracious sakes alive!" cried Mom.

"What's that?" panted Baptista, as she and Carmencita jounced to a stop.

The boys and Dad began to guffaw. Joey lifted her
head.

"Oh," she groaned, "it's Alex!"

Mac quickly let hold of the skinny arm he was still
clutching and looked very sheepish.

"Why did you want to go screeching because you'd
seen him?" he asked Joey disgustedly. "He's not much
bigger than Carmencita."

Alex did look sort of shrunken between the big, richly
tanned twins and tall, sandy Dad.

"I—well, I——" Joey tried to think of a good reason
for her fire whistle scream, "I thought he was a wild
animal. A snake!" she finished triumphantly.

"You did not!" Donny said derisively. "You screamed
'It's Uncle Tom-Tom!' as plain as anything. We heard
you way down by the dam."

Dad scowled. "Superstition" made him even madder
than it did Grandmother. Joey could see he was about
ready to say a few words on the subject when Mom
broke in with her I'll-save-you-now-but-we'll-see-about-
this-later smile, that didn't get as far as the crinkles
around her eyes.

"This is Alex Ryglewicz, our new neighbor," she said
grandly. "Mr. Finch, Donny and Mac Finch, and Baptista Lorenzo. The young lady in the carriage is Baptista's
sister Carmencita."

Much to everybody's surprise, Alex made quite a courtly sweep of a bow. It made Donny and Mac's nods seem almost rude.

Dad smiled at Alex. "Well, the gang grows apace," he said cheerfully. "Before the end of the summer we'll probably have enough for a baseball team."

Alex smiled politely back, but Joey was pretty sure he didn't even know what a baseball team was.

"Say, what were you doing in our woodshed?" asked Donny suspiciously.

Alex looked as if he would like to be back in the woodshed again. "I came to see her." He nodded at Joey. When I saw everyone so busy, I thought I would hide until you had gone. Then I would go home."

Mom broke the embarrassed silence.

"Back to your accounts, Mr. Finch," she said briskly, "and everybody else head for the woods. I've got work to do. Why don't you take Alex along? You've got enough food to feed one more, certainly."

"I have my own food today." Alex proudly held out a tidily wrapped, brown-paper package that was only slightly mashed from the scuffle.

"You'll need it with this tribe of cannibals," said Mom, starting back to the house with her hand in Dad's jacket pocket to steer him.

"Cannibals?" Alex looked at the others for an explanation.

Mac and Donny looked at each other cross-eyed, a favorite signal.

"People that eat each other," said Donny solemnly.

Alex shrugged. "It's a good thing I'm so skinny, then," he remarked gravely.

Donny turned his back on Joey and Baptista's giggles, a surprised look on his face. He hadn't expected Alex to be so quick at catching on to his teasing.

"Let's get going," said Mac.

This time they made it all the way to the Glade without anything serious happening. Maybelle pointed for five minutes at what turned out to be John Rufus's cat, out for a Sunday stroll in the woods, and Princess Joey-Snow Flower walked so slowly in her efforts to be silent that she tripped Baptista up, but that was all.

The Glade was even more fairy-taleish than Joey remembered.

"Look!" breathed Mac as they came quietly down the surveyor's line. Two deer stood at the far edge of the clearing, heads bent over the long grass. In the middle, a brown rabbit sniffed daintily at a stalk of red clover.

"Ha-roo!" Wolf shot past them like a brown cannon ball, and zip! deer and rabbit vanished as if they had never been there, the deer in one long arched jump, the rabbit in a series of frenzied leaps. Wolf snuffled off on their trail, but Maybelle, to the disgust of the twins, flopped down for a nap.

"Okay, everybody, let's get to work." Donny was in his scoutmaster mood. "You girls set up the camp over there under that big elm tree. You'll have to cut branches for beds and clear a big piece of ground for a campfire. Mac and I will have to get a lot done on the shack today. You can help the girls, I suppose," he said carelessly to Alex.

"You can help us unload the lumber first," Mac offered graciously.

Alex walked obediently over to the freight wagon and

started unpiling the boards and planks. Before Joey and Baptista had had time to do more than decide where the beds should go the wagon was clear and Mac and Donny were marking the foundations with a ball of string unrolled between sticks of kindling.

"Aren't we going to find out where the Gray Gull stood?" called Joey. She couldn't see the use of coming clear out here if they weren't going to try to solve the mystery of the old note.

But Mac and Donny were too busy to answer. They had never tried such a large shack before, and they really wanted it to look nice—mainly because they were using new cedar boards instead of old half-painted ones taken from tumble-down sheds around the place. They were fighting over what was the best way to begin. Finally Alex walked over and took the hammer and steel tape out of Mac's hands. He began to wield the two-by-fours, quietly measuring, then pounding in nails with neat, deft strokes of the hammer, and soon a sturdy frame began to appear. Mac and Donny looked flabbergasted, and Joey wanted to cheer. She considered Alex her special responsibility.

Everybody was glad to sprawl under the big elm tree when Joey and Baptista announced lunch—everybody but Carmencita, that is, who had slept all morning and was full of bounces and giggles. They decided to have the ham sandwiches and save the wieners for supper.

Alex unwrapped his sandwiches and laid them neatly on the brown paper on the ground in front of him. Three big slabs, made of grayish bread. Joey looked at *theirs,* Mom's special de-luxers, with the ham ground up with relish and onions and goodness knows what else. She gulped down the hungry taste in her mouth.

"Want to trade, Alex?" she asked, keeping her eyes off those gray slabs. "That's the way we do in school, because everybody gets tired of the same old lunch from home every day. Three of ours for your three."

Mac and Donny started to turn purple, but luckily Alex had his back to them.

"All right," he said finally. "Three for three is fair."

He handed over his sandwiches, and Joey put three lovely ones in front of him.

Then she gave one of the slabs to each of the twins and a ham sandwich each to Carmencita and Baptista.

"Will Carmencita be able to eat this?" she asked doubtfully.

"She eats everything," said Baptista with feeling.

Sure enough, Carmencita began stuffing the sandwich in her mouth with both fat brown hands. Mac and Donny looked considerably less happy about their lunch.

"I'm glad they don't have me alone," Joey thought. "They look as if they'd sure enough like to cut me up in little pieces and feed me to the chickens."

She picked up her own share of Alex's donation. It looked pretty awful, but he'd begin to suspect something was wrong, if one of them didn't start in. So she pretended she was holding her nose and took a big bite. It was like chewing oily white paste and absorbent cotton.

"Lard!" she thought. "Lard sandwiches! Poor Alex."

She looked over at him. His face looked the way Maybelle's did when there were roast beef scraps in her pan. Only a half a ham sandwich remained on the brown paper. He didn't even notice that Donny and Mac were staring at him too.

While Joey watched, both pairs of blue eyes moved thoughtfully to the gray bread in front of them. The lard sandwiches rose slowly in the air. The twins began to chew grimly. Joey grinned.

Nobody complained when she handed out another round of Mom's sandwiches.

Ham turned out to have been a bad choice, though, because it made them all thirsty, and they realized they had only the gallon jug of lemonade to drink until the next morning.

"Next time," said Joey, "we'll bring more water and less food."

She and Baptista were very proud of their morning's work. With Donny's boy scout hatchet, they had lopped nice brushy branches off some of the smaller pine trees near the Glade. Arranged so that they overlapped, with blankets spread smoothly over them, the branches made really expert-looking beds. Even Donny had to admire them.

"Now we have a home in the woods, just like Pineys," remarked Joey.

"Pineys live in dirty old sheds," said Donny scornfully.

Alex and Baptista both looked puzzled. "What are Pineys?" they asked in chorus.

"People who live way back in the woods and swamps. Nobody ever sees them. They're awful." Donny held his nose to show his disgust.

"If no one ever sees them, how are you to know they

are awful?" Alex asked, after a few minutes of anxious
thought.

Donny looked mad, so Mac changed the subject
quickly.

"What are you girls going to do this afternoon?" he
asked. It was plain that he was hoping to get some help
on the shack.

"Dig a hole for the fire," Joey answered hastily.
"Remember what Dad said."

Alex nodded wisely. He never said much, but somehow he listened so carefully that you felt he was part of
the conversation.

As Joey got up to look for something to dig with, her
eye fell on one of the bricks she had found on her first
visit.

"Gee, I wish we could find out more about the Gray
Gull," she complained. "That note we found is driving
me crazy. What *is* the navy of Tarshish?"

"Just like a girl. Wasting her time on some old thing
that happened a million years ago. It's too much like
school for me." Donny gave a long stretch and yawned
loudly.

Alex looked around at the trees. "Where is the
school?" he inquired.

"In Cedarville," Joey explained. "Mom drives us in
every day."

"Ugh! Don't talk about it," begged Mac.

"You'll find out about it yourself soon enough,"
Donny said gloomily. "But you won't have to worry
about being picked on because you're new," he added
patronizingly. "Mac and I are the bosses of the big room

and Joey is the boss of the little room, so you'll be okay wherever they put you."

"Except I won't be in the little room, this year," moaned Joey. The thought made her feel awful all over again. Which was worse, she wondered, living with Grandmother or being in the big room with all those big hulks like Horace Smith and Richard Pettis to tease her when Mac and Donny weren't around?

"What grade will you be in, Alex?" asked Baptista. She was listening openmouthed to this discussion of a two-roomed school.

Alex shook his head. "I have never been to school."

"Lucky thing!" Mac and Donny stared at him enviously.

"You mean you can't read?"

"Or write?"

"How do you find your way around if you can't read signs?"

"How did you learn to speak English?" Baptista spoke last, remembering her mama's and pop's long struggle with the homework from the American Citizenship class.

Alex's nose began to twitch from all this excited questioning. "My mother taught me," he croaked. "She can speak English and read and write. If I learn from her at night, I can help at home during the daytime. When she needs me. Anna is still too little."

"How old is Anna?" asked Baptista interestedly.

"She is four."

"Wow!" Mac rolled over. "I wish I could change places with you."

"So do I," said Alex, swallowing the last bit of his

fifth sandwich. "All my life I have wanted to go to
school."

"Well, you certainly don't need any manual training
class," said Donny handsomely. "Now let's get to work
on the shack. Time's awasting."

Everybody seemed glad to change the subject. Alex
had looked as if he were ready to cry when he talked
about going to school.

Joey and Baptista borrowed short boards from the
boys, and started to dig their pit with those for shovels.
The soft sand flew with practically no work, and they
were coming along wonderfully when Joey's board struck
something hard and jumped right out of her hand, leaving a long splintery scratch.

"Ow!" she yelped.

Luckily, Mac had brought along his scout's first-aid
kit, and he and Baptista, after a lot of bickering over
whether iodine or mercurochrome was better, bandaged
her wound very methodically.

"Just like a girl," said Donny, when the excitement
had died down. "Can't even hold on to a little board for
a second."

"It hit something and got pulled away from me,"
snapped Joey. "Here! I'll show you." Forgetting all about
her hurt hand, she grabbed the board and shoveled out
the sand at her side of the hole.

Mac got down on his stomach. "There is something
there," he reported. "Looks like a piece of a stone wall."

Joey flopped down beside him and began excitedly
to brush the sand away with her fingers. Donny and
Baptista, catching the excitement, started to help, and
soon they had quite a large spot cleared.

"This looks like the foundation to something," Donny said finally.

"The Gray Gull!" screamed Joey. "I told you so! I bet Captain Bones's treasure is buried right here."

But Mac was following the line of the wall away from them, and he shook his head. "It's curving right away," he said. "It seems to be shaped like a horseshoe, and whoever heard of even a piece of a house shaped like that?"

Determined to prove him wrong, Joey scraped away harder than ever. It was no use. The more they cleared, the plainer it was that the stones were indeed forming a horseshoe about three feet across.

"Heck," said Joey finally, "I guess John Rufus is crazy. There wasn't an inn here after all."

"Don't give up so easily," said Mac. "Where are the bricks you said you found when you first discovered the Glade?"

Joey hunted around until she found them.

"The Gray Gull could have been built of those bricks," said Mac reasonably. "That would have made more sense anyway. Where would people have gotten enough stone to build a whole house with in this sandy country? They must have used wood or bricks, same as now."

"Then what is this stone wall?" argued Donny.

Mac shook his head. He didn't have any answer, and no one else could think of any reason for building, besides a house of bricks, a small stone wall in a place where there were no stones. After a while they gave it up and went back to the shack and the fire pit. Joey decided they might as well use two of the rocks for steadying the logs in the fire pit.

"There isn't any other use for them," she muttered crossly to Baptista.

Carmencita slept again, and the boys worked doggedly and silently, pounding nails and sawing boards under Alex's direction. The fun had gone out of the expedition.

Building the fire cheered them up. Donny said to start it when the sun went behind the three tallest elms, and Joey had the sticks and logs ready long before. Mac insisted on trying to light it with stones and tinder, the way they did it in scouts. After he had rubbed the stones together for about the thousandth time, though, Alex asked anxiously if they had forgotten the matches. That brought a laugh, even from Mac, and Donny went ahead and lit the fire with one of the safety matches Joey had brought from home.

Joey showed Alex and Baptista how to spit wieners on a long green stick and roast them slowly over the hot coals. Carmencita, fastened to one of the trees by a long piece of clothes line, waddled happily around in a circle, munching on the potato salad Baptista fed her from time to time.

"Boy," said Mac, stretching out by the fire with a piece of chocolate cake, "this is the best ever."

Everybody agreed with him.

"I wish I didn't have to go," wailed Baptista finally, "but if I don't leave now I'll never make it home by dark."

They helped her pack up Carmencita in the baby carriage and walked with her as far as the Dog Bone.

"You can't miss the way," said Joey. "Follow this trail

till you get to our house, and you know the way from there."

The camping site seemed very quiet without Baptista's gay giggle. And when Alex, with scarcely a word, vanished into the edge of the woods, bound for home and the chores which probably filled his evenings, the three Finches felt completely glum.

"Guess I'll turn in," Mac said finally.

They put out the fire carefully with a few squirts from the extinguisher and rolled up on their piny beds.

Joey watched the stars appear and vanish through the swaying branches of the big elms. She had never realized before that you could hear so many different sounds in the woods. Tiny chirpings and rustlings and crackles, some right in her ear it seemed like.

Her eyes got used to the darkness, and she could see big black shapes against the lighter black that was just air. "Bushes," she told herself, "and trees. That's all."

She wondered what this place had been like with the candles shining from the inn windows, a big stagecoach pulling up at the door. Ladies in red capes like the one in the dress-up trunk got out, helped by tall gentlemen in silk coats and wigs. Then up to the door galloped Captain Bones, his eyes glaring fiercely under the black cocked hat he wore. He cried . . .

Joey sat up. Captain Bones! John Rufus had said his ghost came back to the Glade. What *was* that tall thin black shadow over there? Hadn't it just moved?

"Mac," she whispered, "are you asleep?"

"No."

"What's that shadow over there? The one that's moving?"

"You're seeing things, Joey. There's nothing over there. Wolf would have gone off like an alarm clock if anybody came within a hundred yards of us."

"Not if it was a—a ghost."

"Of all the crazy things." Donny's whisper didn't carry as much conviction as it should have, though. "Let us get some sleep."

Joey's hands felt all cold, even under the warm blankets. "It moved again." She choked. "Closer."

All three of them were sitting up now, straining their eyes to see through the creepy darkness. The shadow moved closer across the clearing. Then, like one of his savage ancestors, Wolf threw back his head and howled.

Joey jumped to her feet, clutching her blankets around her. She was shaking from head to toe.

"Come on," yelled Donny. "Let's get out of here."

Blankets flapping around their legs, the trio stumbled off through the woods. Briars and bushes snatched at the blankets, and once Joey went down flat on her face when her toe caught on a big root. Mac and Donny scooped her up and carried her along at a dead run for a few steps before she found her own feet again. At one point in their mad flight, Maybelle shot past them yowling, but Wolf stuck close to Joey's heels.

On and on they ran. Joey had a stitch in her side that had her bent doubled, and the twins were panting loudly, but they pounded on. Down the Dog Bone, across the dam, and home, where, miraculously, the light was still shining in the living-room windows.

The three of them staggered up the steps, and nearly fell into the living-room door.

"I might have guessed that I would find you in a

shocking state, fleeing from superstitious terrors. I imagined the worst when your mother told me you were camping out."

Joey found just a little breath when she heard the thump of the cane punctuating the familiar voice.

"Grandmother!" she groaned.

8

The Boy in the Holly Swamp

"CAN you see anything?"

"I could before you shoved me. Now I'll have to start all over again." Joey steadied herself by leaning one shoulder against the door and squinted one eye against the keyhole. At first there was nothing but a mist of blue. The corner of the rug. She shifted her gaze upward and picked up the toe of Mom's loafer and tip of Grandmother's cane. They must be sitting on the couch together.

"Well, Louise and Frederic, I hope you are satisfied with the way your children are acting as a result of this dreadful environment in which you have seen fit to raise them. I need not add that their environment is the result of your own rash pigheadedness."

Mom's voice cut into Grandmother's acid speech sharply. "Hush, Mother Finch. The children might hear you."

"Nonsense! They've been asleep for an hour."

Joey, outside the living-room door, smothered a giggle.

"I fail to see how you can possibly have a single reasonable argument to advance in favor of keeping the children here for even one more winter, Frederic. Surely this performance tonight was the last straw."

The tip of the cane twitched violently.

Dad's voice was mild. "The most unsuperstitious person in the world can lose his head in the woods on a dark night. I've seen Uncle Tom-Tom myself on occasion."

"Uncle Tom-Tom! At least he is a real person!"

"For goodness sakes!" Joey nearly lost the keyhole in her surprise at this startling piece of news.

"But to imagine that they have seen a *pirate's ghost*. Really, Frederic, you must see that the tales the people of Cedarville pour out are filling the children's minds with the most dreadful nonsense that they actually

believe. You may be sure they will meet no ghosts in Philadelphia," Grandmother finished firmly.

"What about your great-uncle's bond servant?" Joey could tell from the sound of Daddy's voice that his eyes were twinkling. "You told me he climbs the back stairs every New Year's Eve."

The cane tip bounced angrily up and down. "I told you that story only as a joke, and certainly not when your mind was in the formative stage."

Joey could feel Mac's silent groan as he leaned over her shoulder. If there was one saying they all hated it was "formative stage." Like a tadpole, Donny said once.

But the idea of Grandmother's telling Daddy a ghost story was pretty funny.

Mom's loafer gave a gentle tap. "We mustn't ever forget the good things about Holly River, Mother Finch. The children are tough as nuts by the end of the summer, and the only time Joey has had a cold was after the trip to Philadelphia to stay with you when the boys had measles."

"And so are savages healthy. The school in Cedarville is ruining the children and you know it. The other pupils are ignorant and lazy. How can the children benefit from a school where they never have to sharpen their wits in competition with other alert minds? And," Grandmother added crisply, "they are growing arrogant. Have you noticed how the boys refer to themselves as the 'bosses of the big room' and to Joanna as the 'boss of the little room'?"

Daddy started a chuckle which changed into a cough halfway up his throat. "Not an unusual trait in this family, Mother."

The cane snapped upright. "I see it is useless to continue the discussion if you are going to laugh at my remarks." There wasn't time for anyone to say anything before the black kid slippers joined the cane tip in a march toward the door.

"Quick!" Joey jumped up from her crouch beside the keyhole. The boys, who had been leaning on her, rocked back and just saved themselves in time from falling.

They raced up the stairs in their bare feet, jumping the step at the top (which squeaked), and closed the door of Joey's room, as Grandmother's voice sounded in the downstairs hall.

"Whee!" Mac gave a sigh of relief that whistled all the way up his windpipe.

"All in free," added Donny with a pleased grin.

The banister creaked loudly.

"How are you going to get back to Mac's room?" asked Joey. Donny had surrendered his room to Grandmother. Just as well, as it was clear across the hall.

"Over the back-porch roof," said Mac. "It's only a couple of feet between your window and mine."

"Don't roll off," said Joey. "Grandmother would think that was the last straw to end all last straws."

Joey helped them clamber over the doll house and such books as blocked her window seat. She watched as they crawled slowly over the pale asbestos shingles, their pajamas flapping in the warm breeze. Then she fell into bed and tried to forget all about Grandmother and the terrible threat looming over them.

Mac and Donny were horribly polite at breakfast the next morning, and Joey found herself saying ma'am and sir every time she asked for the butter or another piece of toast. She had put on a dress for the first time since school let out, a pink tucked cotton Grandmother had sent from Wanamaker's. It was so starched that it pricked her neck when she moved her head, but the look of approval from Mom and the snort from Grandmother were worth it.

"Grandmother and I are going to drive to Cape May this morning to see an exhibit of paintings," Mom said, pushing back her coffee cup.

Dad looked up from the paper even Grandmother couldn't stop him from reading at breakfast. "Shouldn't you boys have been at work long ago?"

"John Rufus won't need us until eight because of the extra men, now that the pickers have come," said Mac, inserting his napkin in its ring with fantastic neatness.

"Has he started sanding the new bog?"

"No, we're still grubbing out brush." Donny looked proudly down at the calluses he was getting on his hands.

"There! Donahue said 'bresh' just the way that crude old foreman of yours does, Frederic!"

"Better get going, boys. It's nearly eight," Mom said quickly before Donny could build up steam.

Joey thought Dad was going to build up steam himself, because if there was anyone he admired, it was John Rufus, who had taught him all about growing cranberries when he first bought Holly River years and years ago. But he seemed to be thinking about something else.

"Joey," he said, "where's your atlas?"

"In my bookcase. Why? Did you want to look something up in it?"

"Well, yes. In a way. I'll go up and get it now if you don't mind."

Joey didn't mind a bit, but she thought Dad was acting pretty strange.

"Is there anything you want me to do this morning, Mom?" she asked politely, hoping Grandmother would notice her good manners.

"Well," began Mom, looking at the little pad she sometimes wrote things to do on—and then lost!

"Baptista's on her way in, Joey." Mac stuck his head around the dining-room door. "I met her out back and told her to go in here." Donny gave a loud yell somewhere off and the head vanished—to be replaced by Baptista's black curls.

"I wonder what Grandmother will think of Baptista?"
Joey thought worriedly. Somehow she didn't think they
would hit it off.

But when Mom introduced Baptista, she actually
made a pretty little curtsy in Grandmother's direction.
Grandmother smiled benignly.

"Now that is the kind of manner that was considered
lady-like when I was a little girl. Where did you learn
to make such a charming curtsy, my dear?"

"In dancing class," Baptista said.

Joey looked at her enviously. The only bright spot in
Grandmother's program of Life In Philadelphia was a
weekly dancing lesson. Joey wanted to be a ballet dancer.

"Very nice indeed," said Grandmother, preparing to
leave. "I hope you will teach Joanna some of your pretty
little ways."

Baptista smiled happily and was rewarded with another look of approval when she picked up the mahogany
cane, which had slipped to the floor.

Mom had gone back to the little pad. "How would you
girls like to pick huckleberries this morning? Then I
could make a couple of pies this afternoon."

"Yum!" Joey gave her stomach a happy pat. "Can we
go to the patch near the Holly Swamp? I want to see if
we're going to get good holly and mistletoe this year."

"Yes, the berries are usually best there, anyway." Mom
stuck the pad in the drawer with her napkin and rushed
off to tell Beulah about what there should be for lunch.

"Let's go get the berry pails," said Joey.

Baptista's eyes were round again. "What are berry
pails?" she asked in a rush. "What's a holly swamp? I
thought mistletoe grew at florists."

Her questions tickled Joey, and made her feel important at the same time.

"This is a berry pail," she said going into the pantry
and rummaging out a small tin bucket with a lid that
clamped on tightly. "We tie these strings to the handles
so that we can hang pails around our necks when we
pick and leave both hands free. And I'll show you what
a holly swamp is when we get there. First things first,"
she added, one of Grandmother's irritating sayings.

Baptista pinched her crossly.

Mom came through the pantry. "Better change your
clothes, Joey," she cautioned. "John Rufus says the briars
are simply terrible in the Holly Swamp this year."

"Okay!" Joey tore for her room, Baptista following at a
more sedate pace.

"Boy, am I glad to get into dungarees again!" She
looked at Baptista's neat pink cotton slacks and shook her
head. "You never wear blue jeans, do you?"

Baptista patted her slacks proudly. "No, I love pretty
clothes and nice colors like pink and red."

"I never think about clothes as having *colors*," said
Joey, "just as being comfortable or uncomfortable."

It was Baptista's turn to shake her head. "I guess
maybe it's because you don't have sisters," she decided.
"All I hear at home is whether Bianca's new dress should
be yellow or blue. Even Carmencita cries when we try
to put her into a pair of dark overalls."

"Mom likes to think about clothes, though," said Joey.
"She knows all about colors and things. But she never
talks about them, just buys them."

"That's because the rest of your family isn't interested,

I bet. If she had me and Bianca around, she'd talk about clothes all the time."

"Then I'm glad she doesn't," Joey said firmly, "even though I'd rather have you for a sister than anyone I know."

"I think your grandmother is very nice." Baptista picked up Joey's dress from the floor where she had thrown it and shook it out carefully.

"Ugh! She's all set to take us all back to Philadelphia with her for the winter, that's how nice she is."

Baptista dropped the dress. "Philadelphia! Oh, Joey, I never dreamed there was a chance of your coming to live in Philadelphia. We could do things together all the time if you came."

Joey had never thought about Baptista's Philadelphia and Grandmother's being the same. It was certainly a cheering idea, but not quite cheering enough.

"That would be fun," she admitted, "but I don't ever want to leave Holly River. And I certainly don't want to live with Grandmother."

"Why does she want you to come then?" asked Baptista.

"Because Mac and Donny and I are superstitious." Joey lowered her voice. "We saw Captain Bones's ghost in the Glade after you left last night."

"A ghost! I would have run all the way home."

"That's just what we did do." Joey giggled, for it seemed funnier than it had last night. "And unluckily Grandmother was here when we got home. Boy, was she mad!"

"Because you'd seen a ghost?"

"Because we thought we had. Grandmother doesn't

believe in ghosts, and if anyone else does she thinks they're superstitious and that makes her mad. She thinks Uncle Tom-Tom is superstition, too, only she admitted there is such a person."

"Uncle Tom-Tom!" Baptista had picked the dress up again and was hugging it as if it would protect her from all these awful things. "That's who you thought Alex was, in the woodshed."

Joey blushed. "He's an old man with one red eye who hippity-hops through the woods. He can put a hant on you with his red eye."

"Oh, Joey, let's not go pick huckleberries! Suppose Uncle Tom-Tom found us out there in the swamp? I'm scared to go."

"Pooh," said Joey, and felt as brave as a giant immediately. "He won't get us. Come on!"

The way to the Holly Swamp led past the shanties, deserted today except for Mrs. Lorenzo, who was darning socks and keeping an eye on Carmencita and a bubbling pot of spaghetti sauce. The girls waved as they hurried past, pails bouncing professionally from their belts.

Baptista looked nervous as the road wound deeper into the woods. "It certainly is still, isn't it?"

"No quieter than where we were yesterday," said Joey bravely.

"But the boys were with us then. Joey, you don't think we'll see that *thing* you saw last night, do you?"

Joey wished she hadn't mentioned either Uncle Tom-Tom or Captain Bones's ghost and their scary adventure to Baptista. It was bad enough being half scared to death in the woods herself, but when it came to somebody else's being frightened too——! She tried to give a cheer-ful that's-nothing-but-superstition-laugh, but it came out like a gasp and Baptista jumped right off the ground.

"Tell me about your dancing class," Joey said, to get on a cheerful subject.

"It's wonderful," Baptista said happily. "We learn tap dancing and ballet and do acrobatics every other week."

"Do you go every week?" asked Joey.

"Yes, for an hour. Maybe I can teach you some of the steps. I taught Bianca tap, and now we do a little dance together."

At this glorious possibility Joey was so enthralled with the idea of treating her family to a surprise performance that she forgot all about Uncle Tom-Tom and Captain Bones. She was swinging into a jaunty dance, dressed in a dazzling costume, when Baptista said shakily, "I'm sure someone is following us."

Joey stopped and looked quickly over her shoulder. The road was empty clear back to the last curve, except for the flickering shadows of the oak leaves and a small brown rabbit sitting peacefully beside a fern frond.

"There's no one there now," she said reasonably, "but the road does curve a lot, and someone used to the woods could follow us very quietly by walking on the moss and sand and avoiding the dry leaves."

"Let's go back," begged Baptista.

"Pooh," said Joey. She was feeling braver and braver in comparison with Baptista. "If there had been some-one, Wolf would have barked."

Wolf grinned and wagged his tail, and Baptista, who had forgotten that he was padding along in Joey's shadow, looked braver too.

"Tell me what a holly swamp is," she said.

"Well, that's what we call a swamp that has mostly holly trees growing in it, instead of cedars. We're coming to one now. This is the Maple Swamp dam, and the Holly Swamp begins on the other side."

She and Wolf began to prowl close to the side of the road, looking down at the brush and briars that lined the ditch at the bottom of the embankment.

"Here it is!" she cried, pointing to a plank that lay across the ditch for a bridge. "This is where the path begins."

Joey slid down the bank and balanced her way carefully across the plank. After a minute Baptista followed, and Wolf, disdaining the bridge, jumped after them.

The path was narrower than Joey remembered from when they came up before Christmas to get holly for wreaths. And the briars were really sharp. Mosquitoes hummed over their heads and the black swamp muck squelched underfoot. Then suddenly they were under the towering holly trees and the way was much clearer.

"Where's the mistletoe?" asked Baptista, looking as if she expected to see it spring up in the ground before her.

"Up at the very top of the trees," said Joey, "growing in clumps."

Baptista threw back her head and squinted. "I see it! How in the world do you get it down?"

"Daddy and the twins shoot it down," Joey explained. "They bring their guns when we come for holly and we have a lot of fun seeing who's the best shot. Daddy really is, but Mac's almost as good."

Baptista looked down at her empty berry pail. "Are we getting near the huckleberries?"

"The bushes are right over there beyond the great big holly tree. Come on!"

Picking huckleberries was certainly a dumb job, Joey decided after a while. It was fun at first, but it got so that the more berries you picked, the emptier your pail seemed. Baptista, who hadn't said a word for at least fifteen minutes, didn't seem to mind. She stayed by one bush and stripped it methodically. Joey had to keep looking for bigger berries and thicker clusters, so she hopped around like a sandpiper, stopping frequently to scratch her mosquito bites.

"Where's Wolf?" Baptista asked suddenly.

"Oh, just off chasing a rabbit," said Joey carelessly, with a bravado she didn't feel at all. The swamp was one thing with Wolf lying ready to pounce on the first bad man to come in sight. Without him it was something else again. Something pretty scary.

"Wolf!" she hollered. "Come here, Wolf!"

Her voice echoed lonesomely in the suddenly eerie swamp silence. Then a twig cracked loudly.

"What was that?" Baptista was almost screaming.

Joey clutched her berry pail till her hands hurt. "Wolf!" she shouted desperately. She tried to whistle, but she was so scared that she couldn't make her mouth go right.

Baptista pointed across the little clearing in which they were standing—at a big sassafras bush that was shaking even though there was no breeze in the low hot swamp. Joey felt her legs turn to two lumps of ice. Below the bottom leaves on the bush stood a pair of brown shoes— with feet in them!

There was a crash, and a brown rabbit scooted into the clearing, with Wolf hot on its heels.

"Guard, Wolf," shouted Joey, but her voice didn't shout. It whispered.

Wolf didn't need any order. Right on top of "rabbit," his nose picked up "stranger," and he slammed to a stop. Feet braced, he swung his head toward the bush and began to growl. The rabbit kited for home, but Wolf didn't notice. He was slinking toward the bush, his eyes as red as coals.

Joey summed up some courage she didn't know she had. "You'd better come out," she said shakily, "before my dog jumps you. He's very strong."

What was going to step out from behind that sassafras?

Wolf growled deeply and crouched for the spring. The bush shook, and the brown shoes moved. Joey's eyes opened wide, and Baptista gave a shrill giggle, for a boy stood in front of them. A plain, ordinary boy, about Mac's size, dressed in faded jeans, with faded yellow hair and millions of freckles.

"Well, I'll be!" gasped Joey.

"Where—where did you come from?" stammered Baptista who, after all, didn't expect to find boys lurking behind bushes in what she considered the end of nowhere.

"Over yonder." The boy waved his thumb over his shoulder.

Joey shook her head to see if it was still on. Two strange boys in one summer. It just couldn't happen.

"Do you live where Alex does?" she asked.

"Nope."

"But you don't live too near here, or I would have seen you in school."

"Go to Port Elizabeth. Bus picks me up on the old road, other side of the swamps."

"Well, what do you think you are, sneaking around scaring us this way! If that isn't the meanest thing anyone ever did, I'd like to know it!"

The boy grinned. "Been following you all summer."

Joey gasped. "Why then—you must be Uncle Tom-Tom!"

A funny secret expression took off the grin. Joey thought he looked surprised or frightened or maybe both. She couldn't tell, and in a second the grin was back.

"Nope."

"But you did follow us the night we camped out?"

The grin spread from ear to ear. "Sure did."

"And you were the captain's ghost!"

"Don't know anything about ghosts, but you saw me standing across the clearing and took off like a flock of deer."

Joey began to laugh. Wait till Mac and Donny found

out that they had been chased off by a boy no bigger than they were.

"What's your name?" she chuckled.

"Ted Townsend."

"If you live way back in the swamp, you must be a Piney," announced Baptista, who had been thinking hard during this conversation.

Joey blushed. She wished she had never mentioned Pineys to Baptista and that Donny had not been so scornful in describing them.

"I didn't think Pineys ever went to school," she blurted out, and then wished she'd bitten her tongue in two instead.

"They never used to," said Teddy easily. He didn't seem to mind being called a Piney. "When my parents were kids their parents taught them at home. There weren't any schools handy in those days."

"Why did you start following us?" Joey asked curiously.

Ted flushed. "My brother went in the army," he said slowly. "We used to do everything together. No other kids in the swamps."

"You might at least have come up and introduced yourself," snapped Baptista. "The Finches would have been glad to have somebody to play with!"

Ted shrugged. Joey, knowing how shy Pineys were with strangers, changed the subject quickly.

"Are you good at picking huckleberries? We've got to fill our pails in a hurry and get these back so my mother can make a pie for tonight."

"I'll help."

Ted's fingers flew through the bushes, and the pails were filled in no time at all.

"Why don't you come home with us and meet my brothers?" Joey asked. "I know they'd like to find somebody who could show them how to get through the woods the way you do."

"Like an Indian," said Baptista, rather disapprovingly.

"Okay," said Ted, looking up at the sun. "Show you a short cut."

Ted's short cut was like going through the forest Princess Snow Flower must have seen—down mossy deer paths, over brown creeks slipping secretly through the swamp, and between great oaks and cedars never found by fires or lumbermen. Joey was astonished when she stepped after Ted between two pine trees and found herself on the edge of the orchard not far from the trash dump.

Baptista said good-by and scurried for Little Venice and spaghetti. Ted, carrying Baptista's pail, followed Joey to the kitchen door, where Mom was waiting anxiously for the berries.

Suddenly there was a terrible yell and Mac came racing around the house, his face red as if he was trying to keep from crying.

"Dad's taking Maybelle to the pound," he sobbed.

9
Where is the Gray Gull?

"AT LAST!" said Mom, and then, seeing the stricken faces, added quickly, "but I'm really sorry, Mac dear. What did she do to get Dad so upset?"

Dad, as they all knew, was the last to do anything but laugh when the dogs got into trouble.

"You know how she loves trash? Well, she dumped some old maps and stuff into the wastebasket in the study, and Beulah emptied them into the incinerator." Mac was on the verge of downright blubbering. "Donny's trying to get them out now."

"Great merciful heavens!" Mom sat down hard on the back steps. "Not Daddy's precious maps and deeds?"

"I didn't know Dad had any old maps," said Joey.

"No, you wouldn't. When we first came to Holly River, he was very interested in the history of the county. He was going to do lots of research and then write something on it. He found many old maps and deeds in people's attics, though, and—now they're gone! I don't think Maybelle could have chosen anything worse to turn into trash."

Mac rushed off, and Joey knew he was crying and trying to hide it. She felt like crying herself. Dear floppy Maybelle, the sweetest dog anyone could ever want. But she felt sorry for Dad too. If he had wanted to write about county history those maps must have meant he could do it any day he found the time. Now he'd have to start all over hunting for material, and he'd never be able to duplicate what was lost. No wonder he was mad at Maybelle.

"He bought some diaries from my father," Ted said suddenly.

Joey, who had forgotten all about him, remembered her manners and made introductions. Mom looked pleased.

"I remember your parents well. John Rufus arranged for us to meet them when Mr. Finch started his hunt for old records, because the Townsends have been here since the county was first settled."

Joey was charmed. Here was another lead to discovering about the Gray Gull and its history.

"Why don't you stay to lunch, Ted?" she asked quickly.

Mom seconded the invitation, but Ted refused.

"Still got to look at my rabbit traps today," he said firmly.

Donny came up at that moment, his face and hands black with soot and smoke, and said that while they'd managed to save the diaries and deeds that had covers from the fire, the maps and so on were completely burned up. Maybelle, he reported miserably, was being driven to Court House right after lunch.

Ted looked at him sympathetically. "Come look at my traps. Take your mind off it."

Donny and Mac had been trying to get John Rufus to teach them how to trap rabbits and muskrats for years, and Ted's offer would have turned Donny inside out with delight at any other time. But he just shook his head.

"Thanks, but not today," he said gruffly.

"Saturday, then. I'll pick you up after lunch," Ted offered kindly.

Joey looked at him admiringly. He seemed to be a very nice boy after all.

"Okay," said Donny gratefully. "Want us to bring any special equipment?" He took it for granted that Mac would be included in any invitation.

"Nope." Ted faded into the background like a wary deer, and was gone.

"Can I go with you on Saturday?" asked Joey.

Donny turned on her in a rage.

"Aw for gosh sakes, Joey! Imagine a girl trapping anything. All we'd hear is 'ooh let the poor little bunny-wunny go!' Nuts!"

"I would not!"

"Not what?"

"Make a fuss!"

"Want to bet? You're practically crying now. Ha ha!"

"Donny Finch, you're the stinkiest louse that ever was!"

"It takes one to see one!"

"When I was a little girl I should have had my mouth scrubbed with strong yellow soap for using vulgar words." Grandmother, with Mac trailing glumly behind her, marched out onto the porch and glared at Joey as if she would like to wash her mouth out then and there.

Joey put her head against the porch screen and began to sob loudly.

"Which one of you boys hit Joey?" Dad's head shot

suddenly out of the study window which was next to the
porch along the back of the house. He looked ready to
pop.

"Nobody hit her," said Donny righteously. "She's such
a sissy she started crying for no reason at all."

"What's the matter, baby?" Mom's warm arms came
around Joey's shoulders.

"When I was a little girl——" began Grandmother.

"Mother, please be quiet until we can hear what Joey
has to say," yelled Dad.

The idea of Dad yelling at Grandmother was so enter-
taining that Joey stopped crying.

"Why can't I ever do anything?" She sniffled. "I can't
go trapping or help build the shack or find out about the
Gray Gull or Captain Bones's treasure or anything. And
Maybelle has to go to the pound and we'll never see her
again and I'm just sick of being a g-girl."

Donny started to say something, but Mom shook her
head fiercely at him. Dad leaned his elbows on the
window sill and looked, considering.

"Tell you what," he said finally. "I can't help you about
the shack or the trapping because that's up to Mac and
Donny, and I can't interfere with their business." The
twins looked relieved. "And Maybelle has got to take her
just punishment." Their faces fell. "But finding out about
the Gray Gull is right up my alley. If you want to come
to Court House with me this afternoon we'll go to see a
lady who can put us on the right track in a few minutes."

The mention of Court House, where the pound was,
was enough to break the twins down, and they retired in
misery. When Daddy made up his mind there was no use
whining.

An hour and a half later Dad and Joey set out, with Maybelle, who enjoyed nothing so much as a ride in the car, snuffling happily down their necks, not knowing what lay ahead of her. The twins had gone back to the bogs early to be spared the sight of her final exit.

"Are we really taking Maybelle to the pound?" asked Joey.

"Wait and see," said Dad firmly and then gave her a huge wink. "Let's sing for a while."

He started "My Darling Clementine" and they sang all the rest of the way to Court House, Joey carrying the air while Dad sang tenor. Maybelle seemed to enjoy the concert.

Court House was milling with summer people doing their marketing. Joey was shocked to see that most of the girls had on shorts. Mom and Grandmother stood shoulder to shoulder on what was proper to wear to town. She wriggled inside her pink dress and looked enviously at their bare legs.

Dad pulled up in front of the county offices and announced that he had exactly half an hour of business to take care of. Would Maybelle and Joey care to go across the street for a soda in the meantime? They would, and Joey put Maybelle on the leash and eagerly took the quarter he gave her. The soda tasted so good that she hardly realized the half hour was up when Dad walked in the drugstore and said they had to move on.

They put Maybelle back in the car and walked slowly along the shady street to the county library. Shaded as the street was, the library was so dim that Joey could hardly see. She stood sniffing the delicious smell of warm

leather and book dust, until Dad said, "Mrs. Lindley, this is my daughter Joanna."

A little gray-haired lady no taller than Joey, with the brightest eyes she had ever seen, shook her hand briskly.

"Your father called and said that you were interested in looking up some of the old county history," she said in a voice that made Joey feel comfortable immediately.

"I want to find out about an inn called the Gray Gull that was on the old Cape Road," she explained.

"Of course! Now we have several books written by people who lived long enough ago to have the stories of the early county people at their finger tips. You may borrow those and read through them at home. But while you're here I have a copy of an old surveyor's map that shows the properties in your part of the county."

While she spread the map on the table Mrs. Lindley asked Dad all sorts of questions about Mom and Mac and Donny and even Grandmother.

"Now then," she said finally, "here we are. There is Holly River Creek, and there is the old Cape Road. Show me the spot where you think the inn stood."

Joey traced the old Cape Road with her finger until it crossed a tiny black line that might have been the Dog Bone road. "Between here and Blue Hall Creek," she said. "See, they call it Blue Hall on this map."

Mrs. Lindley put on her glasses and peered at the fine little printing. Joey held her breath.

"Oh yes," said Mrs. Lindley finally. "That was the home of Pork Barrel Reeves, so-called because he rolled a barrel of pork from Cape May to his own house. He wanted to save the expense of hiring a wagon. He was a very close man, and his name became another way of saying 'stingy' here in the county."

Joey let out her breath in a terrible wave of disappointment. If John Rufus was wrong about the Gray Gull, he was probably wrong about Captain Bones and his jeweled peacock. Dad looked disappointed too, but he started to thank Mrs. Lindley very politely.

"The map must be wrong," Joey said suddenly. She

didn't know why, but she was absolutely positive that the Gray Gull had stood in the Glade.

"How could it be?" asked Mrs. Lindley with interest, not as if she thought Joey was a rude little girl.

"I don't know," Joey admitted, "but I bet a lot of those old maps called places by different names than we call them now. I bet Pork Barrel Reeve's house was farther up the Cape Road or something."

"But you said yourself that Blue Hall Creek was the same on the map," said Dad.

"I know," said Joey stubbornly, "but I still think we'll find out someway that the map's wrong."

Mrs. Lindley smiled. "I hope you will," she said, "and I hope you'll let me know what you find out."

"I will," promised Joey. "Thank you very much for the books."

Dad chatted for a few minutes more, and then they left.

The car was clear outside of Court House when Joey suddenly remembered about the pound.

"Aren't you going to take Maybelle to the pound?" she asked.

Dad grinned. "I changed my mind. If you can do historical research with so little to go on, I guess I can start my history of the county without those old papers."

10

A Rainy Day

ALEX and Baptista were both there when they got home, playing kick the can with the twins. Mac, who was "it," hollered "King's Ex" when he saw Maybelle in the back of the car so that Donny could come and rejoice with him. Maybelle was overjoyed to be home, and the three of them whirled like Indians until Alex, who was much more bossy now that he was directing the work on the shack, yelled to them to go on with the game.

Joey joined in without bothering to change her clothes, and they played until Mom called them for supper.

"You've torn your dress," said Baptista reprovingly when the gang collected in the kitchen to wash their hands.

"Who cares?" Joey glared at the rip down the front of the dainty pink cotton.

"I do!" said Mom. "I'll have to mend it."

"Can't you sew?" Baptista asked Joey, her eyes wide and brown.

"Ugh, no!" snorted Joey.

"Not even to make doll clothes?"

Joey gave her hands a final rub with the soap. "That sounds like fun," she admitted.

"It is! I made a whole outfit for my doll just like one I saw in the movies. You should see it!"

"Say, maybe we could make costumes for our dolls for a whole story—the way they do for real plays."

"Oh yes!" Baptista's eyes were shining.

"I've got about fifty dolls up in the attic, I bet. Mom would let us use the material in her scrap box."

"Let's start tonight!" Baptista said eagerly.

"And the boys won't have anything to do with it. We'll show them that we can have fun without them."

Dinner was extra good because it was Grandmother's last night—roast beef, and the huckleberry pie for dessert. In fact, there were two pies, so everybody had all he wanted. Joey was worried about what Grandmother would think of Alex's strange table manners, but he seemed to have become used to the fact that he didn't have to stuff food in with both hands in order to get enough.

And Grandmother paid no attention to the funny way he handled his knife and his fork. Joey decided that there must be something to good manners after all, if they made Grandmother act as if Alex was an important guest and treat him so graciously.

After they had helped Mom with the dishes, Joey and Baptista went up to the attic and hauled out Joey's collection of dolls and carried them down to her room. There were certainly a lot of them, plenty to cast the story of Cinderella, which they had decided to do. There was even an English soldier doll that Grandmother had brought back from Europe. He had an elegant velvet costume and black fur hat, and they decided he could be the prince without any more costuming than a cape.

Grandmother came along when they asked Mom to come up and find the scrap box, and she was so delighted to see Joey playing with dolls that she gave them some good ideas and even offered to send down an old fur collar, which she had in her Philadelphia attic, to trim Cinderella's evening wrap. Joey thought she would rather use the fur to make a rat-coachman, but she had enough sense not to say so.

"But first you have to learn to sew," announced Baptista. "I'm not going to do all the work. You can start with mending your pink dress. I'll show you how."

Joey kicked quite a bit, but Baptista stood fast, and she finally settled down to it. Actually the mending didn't take her long, and Baptista said she was a quick learner.

Grandmother drove off in a sluicing rain on Saturday morning. No more had been said about taking them to Philadelphia, and, on the whole, Joey thought her visit had ended better than it had begun.

"No work this morning," said Mac happily, watching the puddles grow in the road.

"What good does it do us?" grumbled Donny. "We can't work on the shack or go out trapping with that Ted Townsend."

"Where did he come from, Joey?" Mac wanted to know. "I was going to ask you before, but I forgot in all the fuss about Maybelle."

"He's a Piney," Joey explained. "He lives on the other side of the swamps and goes to school at Port Elizabeth. And what do you think? He was what scared us in the Glade that night we camped out."

"He must be some hunter to be able to move around

so quietly that Wolf didn't hear him," Donny said admiringly. He didn't seem to mind having been scared out of his wits by such a good woodsman.

"I'll say. I can't wait to see how he sets traps. Wonder who taught him."

"His brother, I guess." Joey felt important, being the source of all this information. "Ted says he's in the army. I bet Ted will be glad to show you all he knows about hunting and trapping, because he's so lonely now."

"He's a nice guy," Donny stated.

Joey agreed. It was funny how much they all liked Ted, and yet they had seen so little of him. "He doesn't *say* much, but he doesn't need to," she decided, "because you know what he's like from what he's *doing*. Like showing me the short cut and offering to take you trapping."

"We still don't know what to do today." Donny sent a disgusted look toward the window.

"I'm going to see what I can find out about the Gray Gull in those books Mrs. Lindley sent me," said Joey smugly.

"Why don't you boys go help in the barrel house?" suggested Dad, wandering into the living room in search of the morning paper. "John Rufus will be up there working on boxes."

"That's it," cried Joey. "We can try to get some more out of him about the inn. He knows a lot more than he's told us."

Mac, who had looked gloomy at the thought of work, brightened up again. "Good idea, egg head."

"Why bother?" Donny yawned. "You said yourself

there was no inn on that old map at the library. John
Rufus is fooling us with a lot of tall tales."

Joey kept her temper. "There's only one way to find
out, and that's to hear some more from John Rufus. Let's
go."

"Rain in summer is terrible," announced Mac as they
slopped up the hill to the barrel house. "You have to
wear a slicker and then you're boiling hot inside it."

"We ought to wear bathing suits," Joey giggled.

"Not today. This must be a northeast storm because
it's really pretty cold out," said Donny.

He was right because by the time they creaked open
the big sliding door of the barrel house they were glad
to see that John Rufus had the potbellied stove red hot.

"Why, there's Ted," said Joey, yanking off her slicker
hat.

Sure enough, Ted sat cozily by the stove, his chair
tilted and his feet propped on a handy box.

He grinned at their surprise. "I've known John Rufus
longer than you have," he told them.

"Glad to see you," said John Rufus placidly. "Always
do need help with the boxes."

The boxes, which were used to ship the cranberries,
came in pieces from the factory, all ready to join. Nailing
them together was a winter job for John Rufus, or a rainy
day job for summer. While he got the twins set up with
hammers and fourpenny nails, Joey wandered over to the
big whetstone that had a seat like a metal bike seat which
you sat on while you pumped the treadles that turned
the stone. She climbed on the seat and spun the wheel
for a while and then drifted over to the ladder going to

the loft where the barrels had been stored in the old days when cranberries were shipped in barrels.

Climbing the ladder was deliciously scary, and the loft had a good wood smell with the rain beating on the roof as loud as the hammers pounding below her. Joey sat down on a pile of lumber and pulled out the book which she had brought along in her slicker pocket.

The book was harder going than any she had ever read —no pictures and print as small as the words were big. After a while of floundering among long lists of early settlers, she decided it might be easier and much more

fun to get the story from John Rufus, so she clambered
cautiously down the ladder again.

As she pulled up a chair to the stove, John Rufus put
down the box he had just finished joining and pulled an
old black pipe out of his hip pocket.

"Time to take a tempo," he said, meaning "time to
have a rest."

Joey leaned forward and dug her elbows into the tops
of her knees.

"John Rufus," she said coaxingly, "won't you tell us
some more stories about the old days?"

"Please!" echoed Mac and Donny and even Ted.

John Rufus held a match to the old black pipe and
puffed slowly for a few minutes. When smoke was curl-
ing up thickly he settled back in his chair and put his
feet up beside Ted's.

"Things have changed since my grandfather's day,
and that's a fact," he said thoughtfully. "Why, he used to
tell me that what we call Blue Hall Creek was called
Dudley's Run when he was a boy, and there was another
Blue Hall Creek that's dried up now. He called the Blue
Hall 'Dudley's Run' till the day he died."

Joey looked triumphantly at Donny. That explained
why Pork Barrel Reeves's house had appeared to be near
the Blue Hall on Mrs. Lindley's map. "I knew that old
map was wrong," she thought. "If I'd known enough to
look for Dudley's Run instead of the Blue Hall, I bet I
would have found the Gray Gull."

"But what about Tom Bones's treasure, John Rufus?
Did it ever turn up again?" Mac asked softly.

11

The Story of the Gray Gull

YES, yes, it did. A good many years ago.

When my grandfather was a boy, that was how long ago. He was ninety-five when he died, and he and I would sit by the stove keeping an eye on the potpie for my mother when bad weather kept us in. He knew more stories than I do now, and that's saying a lot. But the one I liked best was the one he never told but once—the week before he up and died.

It seems when he was about Joanna's age he used to work for Mr. Edward Dudley who ran the Gray Gull. That was during the 1812 war with the British, and Mr. Dudley, he was all for the English. Most of this part of the county was, being traders and shipbuilders on the Cedar River and thinking there was more money the way the king ran things. But then along in 1813 the British put a blockade all along this coast clear up to New York City, and they began to get mad. No money when their ships couldn't get in or out.

Mr. Dudley stuck right to the king, though, and people began to say nasty things about him. My grandfather, Sam, used to hear the men talking in the public room about how they wouldn't come to the Gray Gull any more, but it was the only tavern around and they had

to meet and talk business and politics somewhere, so that
was only talk. But there was bad feeling, and the word
got around that Edward Dudley might be handing information along to the wrong side.

Miss Betsy Dudley was eighteen that spring of 1813,
and the prettiest girl in the county. Black hair and blue
eyes and a smile and a piece of pie for little Sam. There
wasn't anybody didn't like her, and she was a nice sensible girl too, so when Mr. Dudley found out his brother
was sick up in Philadelphia he hung the key inside the
stable door and took off up the Cape Road without too
much worry. He was sure Miss Betsy would be all right,
what with Sam to take care of the horses and the cow
and Susan Sneed, the hired girl, to help with the cooking
and the customers and look after the chicken yard.

Things went along like cream for a while. Miss Betsy
didn't care about politics, and she served and looked
after the coach travelers as neat as could be.

One night, though, the cream went sour. Sam was
watering the coach horses when he heard Ellis Rice in
the public room, laughing fit to bust. It was warm for
May, and all the windows were opened, so Sam settled
down under one to hear the joke.

"Stewart James, over to Tuckahoe, just pulled the
nicest trick on a Britisher that you'll ever want to hear,"
Ellis was saying. "Seems he tried to run the *Green Lady*
through the blockade into Delaware Bay, and a British
man-of-war sneaked up and captured him. The captain
of the man-of-war put an English midshipman and three
Irish seamen aboard the *Green Lady*, with orders to sail
her to Philadelphia as a prize. This here middy didn't
know anything about navigation and less about the

Jersey coast, so he *ordered* Captain James to steer them to Philadelphia. And then a fog came up."

"James always did have more luck than a rabbit's foot," said one of the other men.

"Naturally Captain James took off for Tuckahoe fast as he could sail the *Green Lady*. And when the fog cleared, that poor simple midshipman found himself in Great Egg Harbor. James pulled a long face and said he was lost because of the fog, so the middy took the knowingest seaman into the cabin to look at the charts. Quick as a wink James hollered that they were running on a reef, and while the other two Irish seamen went for the tiller he locked the cabin door. Three to one is easy odds, and by the time the *Green Lady* reached Tuckahoe all four Britishers were tied up like geese at Christmas."

There was a guffaw of laughter.

"Where are they now?" somebody asked.

"Tied up in Stewart James's shed, waiting for Captain Hughes and the militia to pick them up."

"Has anyone fed them?" asked Miss Betsy's clear gentle voice.

"Who'd waste food on Britishers? We've not got enough ourselves since the blockade and the raids from the British ships." Ellis Rice's voice was harsh.

Sam could hear the rustling of Miss Betsy's skirt as she walked quietly out of the room. He hopped along to the window of her little parlor and peeked in the window, worrying about her. Sure enough, there she was, sitting in her dead mother's rocking chair, holding the golden peacock like she always did when she had a problem or felt sad. Sam never forgot the way the golden bird shone in the light from Miss Betsy's candle.

He went back to the watering trough, and a few minutes later Miss Betsy came out. "Sammy," she said,
"saddle up the gentlemen's horses. I'm closing early
tonight."

It wasn't long before the men were mounting, with a
lot of grumbling at not being allowed to stay later. Sam
could see Miss Betsy and Susan Sneed, the hired girl,
tidying up the public room, and then a candle shone in
the window to Susan's room in the ell. After a few
minutes it went out, and the inn was dark except for a
small light in the kitchen. Sam was about to climb to his
own quarters in the stable loft when Miss Betsy came out
the kitchen door, all wrapped in her red riding cape,
with a saddle bag over her arm.

"Saddle Molly, Sammy," she said. "I'm going to ride
over to Gran Cresse's with some elderberry wine. I'm
afraid she hasn't been getting proper care since this last
bout of rheumatism."

Sam thought Gran Cresse would likely have been in
bed two hours ago, but he saddled up Molly, Miss
Betsy's mare, and helped her to mount. After she had
ridden off he decided not to go to bed. His big toe
prickled like something was going to happen, and he
didn't want to miss it. So he wrapped a quilt around
himself and sat down inside the stable door to wait,
under the hook where the key always hung.

He must have fallen asleep, because when he heard
the sound of Molly's hoofs down the Cape Road the
moon was down. He could tell something was wrong
with the way Molly was trotting, and when he peeked
out the door he saw that there was not one person on her
back but two! Miss Betsy was riding pillion behind a

strange man! You could have knocked Sam over with a
chicken wing.

Molly stopped at the kitchen door, and the man swung
down and then lifted Miss Betsy off. Sam could tell he
thought she was something special, because he handled
her like a dozen eggs. And took longer over the job than

necessary. In the kitchen door they hurried, and a second later a candle was burning in Miss Betsy's parlor.

Sam was trying to get a look through the parlor window when he heard horses down the Cape Road. A lot of them, riding fast. He tore into the inn.

"Miss Betsy," he hollered, "there's a lot of men riding fast in this direction."

Miss Betsy came out of the parlor and shut the door behind her. Her face was the color of her clean white apron.

"Will you do something for me, Sammy, something that you must never tell a living soul?"

If Miss Betsy had told Sam to tie a flatiron to each foot and jump into the Cedar River he would have done it, so he nodded hard.

"I'm going to talk to the men by the front door. I want you to take the gentleman in the parlor out to the hen house. When you hear me call your name, let the hens out. Be sure and stir them up so that they fly around. Then take the gentleman and run for the bog as fast as you can. Hide him under the bank where you tether Sukey, and then get back here fast. I want you to climb up to your loft and come down again as if you had been asleep all the time and didn't hear me call you. Can you do that, Sammy?"

Sam nodded again. He knew he had it clear.

Miss Betsy patted him on the shoulder and then knelt down and hugged him. "I knew you could!" she said warmly.

Then she was running toward the front door.

The gentleman must have been listening at the parlor door, because he came right out and stood waiting for

Sam to lead him to the hen house. It was too dark for Sam to see at that moment, but he got a look at the stranger later. He said he was young, with a thin face and long nose and very light hair.

"Lead on, heroic lad," the stranger said. He had a funny way of talking, too, Sam said.

They reached the hen house about the time the riders reached the inn door. They reined in, and Sam could hear the bolt creak as Miss Betsy opened the door.

"Good evening, gentlemen," she said sweetly. "This inn is closed for the evening, and I am about to retire. I should be pleased if your business could wait until morning."

"Well, it can't," said Ellis Rice's harsh voice. "This here is Captain Hughes, and he's after an escaped Britisher."

"Why waste time here? The Gray Gull is closed, and has been for hours."

"There were four Britishers in Stewart James's shed. Tied hand and foot with seamen's knots. Somebody came there tonight and cut the ropes with a knife. When Captain Hughes and his men arrived Stewart James took them down to the shed. They found the men were gone and spread the alarm. We caught the three seamen. They hadn't gotten far. But the midshipman has clean vanished. He must have gotten away on a horse. And somebody saw you ride into Tuckahoe tonight, Miss Betsy."

"Whoever saw me was mistaken," said Miss Betsy quietly. "I have not left the inn tonight. However, since my father's loyalties seem to lay this house under suspicion, I beg you will search the inn immediately so that we may be cleared of all suspicion."

The militiamen coughed and cleared their throats as if they were embarrassed. Everyone liked Miss Betsy, and she spoke so sweetly and sincerely that it seemed downright silly to think she had freed four British sailors and ridden off with one of them.

"Now, ma'am, I don't think we need to——" began Captain Hughes.

But Ellis Rice interrupted him. "Not the inn. She'd not be fool enough to hide him there. The stable is the place, and the sheds. We'll look there."

"Very well. I will have the boy take your horses." Miss Betsy made her voice high and clear. "Sam! Sammy Leaming! Come here!"

Sam tore open the hen-house door and began poking the hens with a stick. The stranger helped him with a will, and before long they had to cover their faces with their hands to escape the flying claws and feathers. The squawking was enough to break an ear open. Out the door poured the hens, and filled the yard with their mad flappings.

"A fox!" cried Miss Betsy. "Gentlemen, please help me

catch my hens before the fox makes off with one of them."

The militiamen were gentlemen, and Miss Betsy had a mighty pretty face. They were down from their horses and dashing after the fat birds before Ellis Rice could open his lips. And between the shouts of the men and the squawks of the hens they couldn't hear him after the chase began, not if he bellowed like a bittern.

Sam grabbed the gentleman's hand and ran for the bog. He led Sukey the cow through the woods every morning and every night, so he knew the way with his eyes shut. The gentleman was a fast runner and as light on his feet as a wildcat, so they reached the bog in no time.

Under the giant cedar where Sukey was tied there was a muskrat hole about halfway down the bank of the bog. Sam had dug it bigger, because it made a handy place to leave pails during berry season and such, and also a good hide-out when he felt like taking a nap. He told the gentleman to climb down into the hole and then ran back to the inn.

Miss Betsy had told him to get up in the loft again, but he wasn't going to do that—not with a mean man like Ellis Rice hanging around. No telling what he might decide to do next. The soldiers had got all the hens back in the coop and were beating the bushes for the man they were looking for. Sam was a boy whose head was in the right place, and he had a pretty good idea that the midshipman from the British warship was fighting mosquitoes in the muskrat hole right this minute. But he was on Miss Betsy's side, whichever that was.

He got up under the public-room window, but Miss

Betsy must have drawn the curtains because he couldn't see anything. He heard a man's boots thump into the room and then Ellis Rice began to bellow.

"No use looking for the Englishman. You know and I know that he got away in the confusion. Very clever, Miss Betsy Dudley, nearly as clever as your traitor father."

"Take care," said Miss Betsy, and her voice wasn't gentle now. "You have no proof by which to doubt the loyalty of this house."

"No indeed. And therefore I'm assuming that you're for the United States of America." Ellis Rice was talking soft now, like he did when he was selling dried-out cedar blocks to an outlander. "Of course, all the patriotic people have given a contribution to the Cause, as much as they could spare. We haven't collected from you and your father, but this is as good a time as any."

"I have no ready cash," said Miss Betsy calmly. "No more than a handful of silver."

"I was thinking of the pirate's peacock," said Ellis Rice in the oily voice he used when the deal was all but signed on.

Sam nearly fell off the rain barrel. He had often heard Mr. Dudley saying that the peacock was a Sacred Trust, to be kept for the day when a descendant of Captain Tom Bones would come to fetch it. The peacock, he would say, was not his to sell or give away.

"That's fair enough," said Miss Betsy, just as if she was taking a length of calico after a bit of dickering. "I'll call Captain Hughes to come in and witness the bargain."

Sam could hear her heels tapping to the door and her

voice echoing the captain's name through the night.
Captain Hughes and his men all came immediately, as if
they knew it was useless to go on searching.

"You must be thirsty after such hard work," Miss Betsy
said when they had straggled into the public room.
"Mr. Rice's business will wait until I have mixed a cool
drink, I feel sure."

Ellis Rice growled. It was easy to tell he didn't like
the way things were going, but Captain Hughes got his
words in first.

"We should be honored, Miss Dudley," he said
gallantly.

Tap, tap went Miss Betsy's shoes again, this time to
the kitchen. Ellis Rice started dressing Captain Hughes
down about the way he had failed in his duty by letting
the midshipman get away. Captain Hughes got angry
and told him off right back. Ellis was plainly spiteful,
he said, and probably just led them to the Gray Gull for
no reason other than to get Miss Betsy in trouble. He
was sure the midshipman had escaped by boat and was
safe on a British ship by now. Sam thought they were
going to start fighting, but then Miss Betsy came back
and Captain Hughes was too much of a gentleman to
fight in front of a lady.

Glasses tinkled, and the Captain and Miss Betsy
chatted as if they were at a tea party. When they got
through the weather and started on the price of tea and
coffee Ellis Rice set his glass down with a crash.

"Enough of this tattle," he yelled. "Give us that bird
and we'll be off."

"I am so sorry," Miss Betsy said sweetly, "but I am

afraid my father must have taken it with him for safe-keeping. I am unable to find the peacock anywhere."

Sam knew this was an out-and-out fib. He'd seen Miss Betsy with the peacock in her hands not two hours ago. Evidently Ellis Rice knew it was a lie too, because he began demanding to search the inn.

"You're overstepping yourself, Rice," snapped Captain Hughes. "Even if the jeweled bird were here, you have no authority to take it. Miss Dudley, we have trespassed on your hospitality too long and will bid you good night. Our thanks for your generosity and courtesy."

And with that he marched out of the public room and out of the front door, followed by Ellis Rice who was being helped along by a couple of tall sergeants, one on each side of him. . . .

John Rufus stirred and blinked as if he had been asleep. He knocked his pipe on the potbellied stove and nodded toward the window.

"Rain's over. Better be out and stirring your stumps."

"But what's the end of the story?" screamed the three Finches and Ted in unison.

"That's the end of the story. My grandfather went to bed up in the loft and slept till the sun came up. In the morning he found that Miss Betsy had gone away during the night, and so had her mare and Edward Dudley's big chestnut stallion. She had left the key inside the stable door, the way the Dudleys always did when they went on a trip. Grandfather ran down to the muskrat hole, and that was empty too. All except for a note in Miss Betsy's hand, pinned to her red riding cape so that he wouldn't miss it."

Joey rushed over and grabbed John Rufus's arm. "What did the note say?"

John Rufus shut his eyes again, remembering. "It appears to me like Granddad never told me," he said finally.

"I know what it said," cried Mac, "and it's sitting in Joey's atlas this minute."

"Of course!" yelled Donny. "The note on the bill of sale we found in the red cape. Our red cape must have belonged to Miss Betsy Dudley. It all fits in!"

Everybody was stunned by this discovery except Ted, who of course didn't know about the red cape, and John Rufus, who seemed to be dreaming again.

"But how did Miss Betsy's red cape get into our attic?" Joey wanted to know.

Mac shook his head. "One more mystery to solve."

"And how did the note get into the pocket of the cape if Miss Betsy left it for her father? John Rufus, would your grandfather have put the note in Miss Betsy's riding cape?"

John Rufus came out of his dream. "Why that's just what he did do, Donahue. Sam and Susan Sneed waited for a whole month for Edward Dudley to come back from Philadelphia. Then they heard he was never coming back. Miss Betsy and the midshipman had been married by the captain of the British ship they managed to board in the Delaware Bay the night they ran away. Seems like they had fallen in love at first sight and didn't want to take a chance on being parted again." (Joey sighed romantically.) "And what with the hard feelings back in the county against people who sided with the British, Edward Dudley decided not to go back to the Gray Gull. As soon as his brother was well he went up to Canada and sailed to England to join Miss Betsy and her husband."

"And what did your grandfather do when he heard that?" asked Ted.

"He helped Susan Sneed pack up Miss Betsy's clothes in case she should send for them. He must have put the note into the pocket of her riding cape for safe-keeping. Then he and Susan Sneed went off to their own homes."

"What about the peacock?" Joey was bouncing with excitement. "Was that ever found?"

"Folks said Miss Betsy took the peacock when she ran off, and maybe she did. Mr. Dudley's nephew, the son of his Philadelphia brother, came down and took over the Gray Gull a few years later. He knew about the peacock, and he and his family after him wasted a good deal of time tearing up the floor boards, but they never found it. Seems as if they would have located it if it had been there."

"What did your grandfather think?" asked Ted shrewdly.

"That Miss Betsy hid it when she went to get the drinks, so that Ellis Rice couldn't steal it. But the family liked to blame all their bad luck on Miss Betsy's taking the peacock. The Gray Gull was never the same. Finally, when the roof fell in one winter, the Dudley tribe went back to Philadelphia, and the inn just gradually collapsed."

"Come on!" Joey was ready to turn inside out. "Let's go right to the Glade now and start looking."

12

Digging for Treasure

"Shovels," said Ted practically.

"And let's look at the note for any further clues," said Mac. "Now that we know the whole story."

"Personally," said Donny, "I think this is a waste of time."

Everybody stopped short in their tracks and stared at him, Joey fiercely, Ted and Mac doubtfully.

"Why?" asked Mac finally.

Donny shrugged. "If the peacock was still there— and remember, we don't really know if there ever was a peacock—the Dudley family would have found it years ago. Either they found it and sold it, or Miss Betsy took it when she ran away. Either way, it's no use our looking for it."

"Miss Betsy wouldn't do that!" snapped Joey. "She'd never take the bird if it was a Sacred Trust."

But Ted and Mac looked as if they agreed with Donny.

"We don't know what Miss Betsy was like," said Mac reasonably.

"I do," said Joey stubbornly, "and if you won't come with me I'll go dig up the Glade by myself."

She marched off down the road past the packing house, and after a minute the boys tagged along. They

still weren't convinced, but they plainly didn't want Joey
to find the peacock and then hog all the glory.

"Baptista and Alex are waiting for you," said Mom a
little crossly when they stormed through the door into
the kitchen.

Joey blushed. She had told Baptista to come over this
afternoon without fail and then had gone off and forgotten her.

"I thought you might like to work on the Cinderella
costumes some more," Baptista said. She and Alex had
been looking at old copies of the *National Geographic*
in the sitting room. "Bianca gave me a big piece of tulle
for Cinderella's wedding veil."

"Forget about that," ordered Joey. "We've got something really important to do. We're going up to the Glade
to look for a jeweled peacock. John Rufus told us a lot
more about the Gray Gull and the mystery. Come on!"

"Don't you boss me around, Joey Finch!" Baptista's
eyes were hot with temper. "I don't happen to want to
go off in those nasty buggy woods again. I want to stay
here and play dolls, like you promised you would."

"Don't be silly!" Joey snapped impatiently. "This is
going to be a lot more fun. Put that tulle somewhere,
and we'll get started."

"I'll get started home! I don't want to go anywhere
with a bossy thing like you." Baptista marched toward
the door, then stopped for a parting shot. "If I wanted
to dig, I could go out on the bogs and get paid for it.
Did you ever think of that, smarty?"

Joey swallowed. "Smarty." "A bossy thing like you."
That sounded like Evelyn Smith and, what was worse,
like what Mom had said about Grandmother.

"I'm sorry, Baptista," she said miserably. "I'll stay and play dolls if you want, and I promise not to be bossy."

Ted looked at the two girls calmly. "Baptista doesn't have to dig," he said. "Once we've figured out where the treasure is we're only going to need one shovel to get to it."

Joey felt very relieved by this sensible compromise. "Thank you," she whispered gratefully to Ted. He winked at her understandingly.

"If we find the peacock, Baptista," wheedled Mac, "you can buy all sorts of things for your family with your share of the money."

"What money?" asked Ted.

"Why, we'll get Grandmother to take it up to Philadelphia for us and sell it. We'll be rich."

Baptista smiled at the thought of such splendor. "I'll go," she announced.

"Wait until I go up and get the note on the bill of sale," said Joey.

She tore up the stairs and went straight to the biggest shelf on her bookcase. The atlas wasn't there. Joey was sure she hadn't used it since they found the bill of sale, but one of the twins might have wanted to look for something on the maps. She was going to call down to them, when she saw the atlas lying on its side on the window seat.

"Dumb boys," she muttered, shaking it open.

The bill of sale was gone. Joey shook the book and finally went through it page by page, but the yellow scrap was missing.

Joey shivered as if she had jumped in the ocean on a cold day. Who could have taken the bill of sale? Mac

or Donny would have mentioned it downstairs if they
had taken it for any reason. Maybe Miss Betsy herself
had been looking for it. Suppose it wasn't Captain Bones
at all who haunted the Glade, but Miss Betsy! Suppose
she was even haunting Joey's room, looking for her note!

Feeling an urgent need for lots of company, Joey
raced down to the living room.

"Mac or Donny, did you take the bill?" she demanded.
Her voice sounded trickly, and the other four looked
surprised.

"Gosh no," said Donny. "Don't tell me you've lost it,
stupid. We might have known you would."

"Stupid yourself!" raged Joey. Losing the bill and then
getting so scared seemed to have started a kettle boiling
inside her.

"It takes one to see one," mocked Donny, his eyes
shining meanly.

Even Baptista couldn't let that pass unchallenged.
She tossed her head and said scornfully, "Speak for
yourself, Donny Finch."

"Yes," snapped Joey, "people in glass houses shouldn't
throw stones."

"Is it not believable that you would put it in another
book by mischance?" asked Alex, before Donny could
open his mouth to produce another dig.

"Nope," said Joey firmly. "I remember the atlas dis-
tinctly. Daddy asked me where I had put it, and I told
him." There was something else about Daddy wanting
the atlas at the back of her mind, but she couldn't
remember what it was.

Baptista shook her glossy curls confusedly. "Who
would have taken it?"

"Maybe Miss Betsy's ghost did," whispered Joey.

The others looked as if *they* had all jumped into a frigid ocean. There was a long, trembly silence.

"Pooh," Mac said finally, and then started nervously at the sound of his own voice. He rallied and went on. "We all know there's no such things as ghosts."

Baptista's eyes were like saucers. "Where my mother was a girl in Italy," she announced, "the palace of the prince had not one ghost, but sixteen."

Joey groaned. "I'll never be able to sleep in my room again. And I certainly can't go back to the Glade."

"Ghosts are unable to walk in the daylight," said Alex.

"Don't be a bunch of scaredy-cats," said Donny. "Let's get going."

Because nobody wanted to be a scaredy-cat they trailed off to the tool shed in search of shovels.

Joey had never seen the woods so silent. Even the mosquitoes had stopped buzzing, it seemed, but not biting. She scratched thoughtfully. Where would Miss Betsy have hidden the peacock?

"Better see if we can find the foundation of the kitchen fireplace," said a voice practically in her ear. Joey leaped right off the ground.

Ted had come up beside her as quietly as smoke and was walking silently, close at her side.

"I wish you'd stop sneaking around," said Joey irritably.

Mac turned around. "Why the fireplace?"

"Likeliest place to have a hideyhole."

"And she did go in the kitchen," Joey added eagerly, "to get the drinks. John Rufus said so."

"I wish you'd tell me what this is all about," pleaded Baptista. "Alex and I still haven't heard the story."

Joey started in, and what with Mac and Donny and Ted interrupting and correcting her, and having to stop and explain more slowly to Alex they were at the Glade before she had finished.

"My goodness!" Baptista looked at the sleepy green clearing with amazement. "Imagine all that happening right here!"

"Let's get to work," said Mac practically.

"Look for stones and bricks," said Ted. "No use to start digging until we find the best place."

Joey started at the spot where she had uncovered that funny horseshoe-shaped stone wall, and the others spread themselves out in an uneven rectangle around her.

"Here's a brick!" called Baptista.

"And another," from Mac.

"And here a small piece of wall," bragged Alex.

But as the afternoon dragged on and it became hotter and itchier by the minute in the Glade they stopped talking. It seemed as if the rest of their lives would be spent inching along the ground like big robins, plunging occasionally after a brick instead of a worm. Crawl until the cramps in your back got unbearable, stand for a minute to stretch them out, then crawl again.

Joey stood up for what felt like her ninetieth stretch and looked sleepily around at the others.

"Yowee," she squealed suddenly. "I can see the shape of the Gray Gull!"

All but Ted jumped to their feet and looked with her. Sure enough, there was a surprisingly recognizable floor

plan marked out by the grubby bits of brick that lay around the clearing.

"This long room across the front was the public room," Joey cried.

"And I bet that small one behind was the parlor."

"And the bigger one behind must have been the kitchen. They were always big rooms," finished Donny, with his best know-it-all look.

Alex looked thoughtfully at Ted. "What do you think?" he asked.

"Fits my idea of the layout." Ted nodded. "We better concentrate on the kitchen part now."

Joey started scrabbling along the line marking the kitchen walls with new energy. She was a great archaeologist now, digging up the walls of Pompeii. Daddy had read an article about excavating to them last winter.

Suddenly she realized she had reached her starting point, the stones she had found digging the fire hole. She picked one up and glared at it. "Why can't you talk?" she muttered crossly.

Where had she seen a stone like that before, all black along one side? Then she knew.

"In the fire hole. The stones we used to brace our fire got all black along one side like this. This funny-shaped wall must have been the kitchen fireplace." She was screaming with excitement.

Mac grabbed a shovel and came dashing to where she was squatting. The others weren't far behind him.

"What morons!" exclaimed Donny. "The fireplace was right under our noses from the very first day, and we didn't even recognize it. Peacock, here we come!"

But an hour later he sat down in discouragement.

"It just isn't here," said Baptista tiredly, looking at the big empty pit they had dug.

Mac plunked down beside Donny. "Those old Dudleys must have found the peacock after all."

"Miss Betsy took it," said Donny maliciously.

Joey was too tired and disappointed to argue.

"It's got to be here," she moaned.

"Well, it's not. We'd better get along home. It's getting late." Mac looked apprehensively at the shadows flowing from the tall elms and walnut trees.

Ted frowned at the gaping hole. He had been so *sure*.

"What's that?" Joey's voice shook.

In the listening silence, a low creaking sounded at the other side of the darkening clearing.

The six of them huddled hastily together.

"Just an old grapevine swinging in the wind," said Ted calmly.

Joey shivered. She didn't for a minute think that creak was a grapevine swinging, and she could tell from the frozen way the others were sitting that they didn't either. And it wasn't Ted, like before, because he was sitting right beside her.

Maybelle whined uneasily, and Wolf gave a soft growl and inched nearer to Joey.

"The sassafras bush over there is moving," whispered Baptista.

"The wind," said Ted, but he didn't seem so calm now.

Joey could see the whites of Alex's eyes shine as he looked slowly around the Glade.

"None of the other trees so much as stir," he said softly.

The sassafras bush shook harder, the creaking sounded louder, and Joey felt that she would like to dig a hole and run into it, like a chipmunk.

"Miauw!"

Wolf and Maybelle jumped up with delighted howls, and were off in pursuit of their favorite enemy.

"John Rufus's old cat!" said Donny disgustedly. "She was in that sassafras bush the whole time."

"It creaked when she moved in it." Ted grinned. "That was the noise that scared us so."

"We sure are scaredy-*cats*." Mac chuckled at his own pun. "We'd better get out of here before Maybelle starts frightening us."

It was a sad-looking group that trudged back down the Dog Bone and over the Brook Bog dam. Dirt from digging seemed to be everywhere, hands, faces, clothes

—Joey could even feel it in her hair. And the thought of that empty pit where the horseshoe-shaped fireplace had been put glum faces on everyone.

"If Joey hadn't lost our only clue we might have found the peacock by now," Donny grumbled.

"How many times do I have to tell you somebody took it?" Joey said hotly.

"Let's not start an argument," said Mac gloomily. "Not if we want to ever get out of the house again before we're shipped to Philadelphia. There's Grandmother's car in the driveway."

Donny groaned. "We'd better say good-by here."

Alex, Ted, and Baptista watched pityingly as the Finches trotted dismally toward home.

"As if we were going to Pompeii, knowing that Vesuvius was going to start pouring red-hot lava down on us as soon as we got there," thought Joey.

"We may be able to sneak across the front hall and up the stairs without being seen if we don't turn the light on," said Donny. "We're all wearing sneakers."

"Good idea." Mac slipped up behind the big forsythia bush near the living-room window to scout. "I think they're all in the living room," he reported. "I could see the top of Mom's head and Dad's back, and I *think* a black spot was the feather on Grandmother's hat."

"Is the door closed?" asked Joey.

"Yes."

"Then we've got a chance."

They slid up the front steps and eased the screen door open and closed. Joey tiptoed across the hall behind Mac, her heart beating like a drum. The mat, the rug, the bottom step. Almost safe. But at that moment, the

sitting-room door swung open and caught them in a flood of light. There stood Grandmother.

"Filthy," she snapped. "Louise, come and look at these children."

Mom stood beside her. At the sight of Joey her shoulders sagged. "Grandmother brought you a lovely new dress, Joey. Scrub off that dirt if you have to use sandpaper and put the dress on for dinner. And you might as well throw those jeans out. I seriously doubt if they'll ever come clean enough to use as dust rags."

The kettle started boiling in Joey's chest again. Why did she get all the blame and the twins none? It wasn't fair, fair, *fair!* Nobody told them to put on a hateful dress or throw away their blue jeans. She stamped upstairs and into the bathroom and started the tub with a roar. Sandpaper indeed!

The bath should have felt good after the sticky woods, but it didn't. The soap made Joey's mosquito bites sting, and her chigger bites came up in great itchy red bumps in the hot water. She slipped getting out of the tub and cracked her elbow on the faucets. By the time she got back to her room tears were running down her face.

There on the bed lay the *dress*, pink, of course, and scratchy organdy, of course, with tight sleeves and a high, hot neck ruffle, of course. The lid blew right off the kettle. Joey ran for the bureau and got her scissors.

The whole family was sitting at the supper table when she marched down the stairs and into the dining room. There was a stricken gasp and then an awful silence.

"Joanna," said Grandmother finally, "what have you done to that dress?"

Her voice sent a shiver right into Joey's toes.

"I cut off the sleeves," she whispered.

"That is apparent. And the collar. *And* the flounce around the bottom. And why, may I ask, are you wearing what appears to be a cotton nightdress beneath it, instead of a proper petticoat?"

Joey swallowed hard. "It scratched me."

"I see."

"Go to your room, Joey," said Mom. Her voice was worse than Grandmother's. "We'll talk about this later."

Joey scuttered for the stairs. When she reached the door to her room, she stopped and listened because she thought her ears must be fooling her. It sounded as if Dad was laughing.

He certainly wasn't laughing when he brought her dinner up an hour later.

"Mom's trying to keep Grandmother from going straight back to Philadelphia tonight," he explained.

Joey nodded and pitched into the cold chicken and corn bread. She was too hungry to talk.

Dad watched her for a minute and then sat down on the window seat. "That was a mean thing to do, Joey," he said. "Grandmother put a lot of time and thought into getting that dress because she wanted you to like it. How would you have felt if I cut up that tie you gave me for my birthday?"

"The tie wasn't scratchy," said Joey through a chunk of corn bread.

"Don't talk with your mouth full. I might not have liked the color, but I wouldn't have said so. I'd have worn it anyway, to give you the pleasure of thinking you'd given me a present I liked."

Joey licked a bare bone regretfully. "I sort of thought

Grandmother bought me dresses I didn't like on purpose."

Dad grinned. "Your Grandmother is an iron woman, but she's not a mean one. You can take my word for it that she thought you'd really like that dress."

Joey scraped her plate and looked consideringly at the opposite wall. "Then I'm sorry," she said finally.

"Right. Let's go and tell Grandmother so." Dad went over to the closet. "Only you'll have to put on something presentable. Here." He hauled out a dress and threw it to Joey, who started to laugh.

"Grandmother would drive herself to Philadelphia if she saw me in this. Mom calls it my Orphan Annie dress."

She hung up the dress, an old school one made of faded gingham, and pulled out her favorite, a gay red and green plaid cotton.

"Grandmother gave me this one too," she explained. "I don't mind this kind of dress, only ruffles."

Dad studied her while she buttoned the dress. "That's because you look terrible in ruffles and nice in this," he announced.

Joey smoothed down the skirt, feeling pleased. "You mean I have good taste?"

"That's it exactly. Now let's go cheer Grandmother."

Joey just had to giggle at that.

Grandmother looked pretty fierce when they walked into the sitting room, but Dad didn't give her time to say anything.

"Joey and I have made a discovery," he said seriously. "She has excellent taste in clothes. Her ruinous assault on the pink dress in question was merely an attempt to alter it to suit her style. This dress is her style."

Grandmother didn't blow up. She looked piercingly at Joey, who said, "I'm sorry, Grandmother," in a small voice.

"You're absolutely right, Frederic," Grandmother said briskly. "Joanna clearly has good clothes sense and that pink dress would have been impossible on her. From now on, she shall pick out her own dresses."

Joey felt as if she had been given a prize. Imagine picking out dresses that didn't prickle and coats that didn't pinch. It was too good to be true. And the thought of having "good clothes sense" was exciting. Wait till she told Baptista that. She beamed at Grandmother, who smiled right back.

13
Grandmother Helps

"We're all going visiting this afternoon," announced Mom, as she started to stack the lunch dishes.

There were three loud groans, and then the twins' faces cheered simultaneously.

"Have to work," said Mac. He was starting to imitate Ted's abbreviated way of talking, as well as his woodsman's ways.

"Dad has arranged with John Rufus to let you off. The new bog is nearly finished, and there won't be much extra work from now until picking."

"Then we have to go fishing," protested Donny. "The catfish are biting good over in the Blue Hall."

"Such English!" teased Mom. "I believe Grandmother is right about your going away to school."

The ghost of Grandmother, who had departed in state that morning, filled the room ominously.

"Okay," said Mac quickly. "We'll go."

"I hate visiting," grumbled Joey. "Being patted on the head and told you look bigger or smaller, and then sitting listening to grownups talking all afternoon. Gosh!"

"I think you'll enjoy this visit," said Mom. "We're going to see Alex's mother and father."

Joey walked slowly into the kitchen. Vangie Smith's

descriptions of the way "Polacks" lived echoed in her mind. She liked Alex, but he probably wasn't a real "Polack." But those lard sandwiches stuck in her memory.

"I guess I won't have to change my clothes, will I?" she said.

Mom was surprised. "Of course you will. Imagine going visiting in those dirty jeans!"

"Po——The Ryglewiczes are dirty, I bet."

"Alex is always a great deal cleaner than any of you three," said Mom dryly, "not that that's any standard. Mrs. Ryglewicz wouldn't have a very high opinion of our household if she saw you right now."

But Joey's nose remained wrinkled as she washed her face and hands and climbed into the plaid dress.

"I don't blame the Ryglewiczes for not going into society if it's as hard to get out of their place as it is to get in," remarked Dad as the car bumped slowly into a small bare-dirt farmyard.

"Those must be geese!" cried Joey. "I've never seen any before. Do they hurt people?"

"Not if people leave them alone," said Mom, climbing bravely out of the front seat. Joey noticed she gave the hissing geese a wide berth, though.

"I'll knock," cried Mac, tumbling out after her. "Gosh, what a neat house."

Joey looked at the little building curiously. In contrast to the homes of Cedarville, which were shiftlessly left a wormy, unpainted gray, it was a cheerful red. Much nicer than their plain old white with green trim. She followed Donny out of the car and kept a weather eye on the geese, while Mac thumped on the front door.

"Someone's looking out of the front window," whispered Donny.

The checked curtain twitched gently, and Joey saw a glimpse of dark eyes and a very white face. She felt uncomfortable. Then the door opened slowly, and a square, gray-haired woman stood carefully in front of it.

"Yes?" she said softly.

"Mrs. Ryglewicz?" asked Mom.

The woman nodded.

"I'm Mrs. Finch from Holly River, and this is my husband. These are the children who play with Alex all the time, Joey, Mac, and Donny."

Mrs. Ryglewicz looked at them intently. Her eyes reminded Joey of Alex's that first day by the trash dump.

"Please come in," she said finally.

Joey's nose started wrinkling in anticipation, but when she stepped inside it smoothed itself out in a hurry. This was the cleanest room she had ever seen. The walls were rough, like the inside of John Rufus's hen house, but they were whitewashed and clean as snow. There was a big table in the middle of the floor that looked homemade, covered with gay red and white oilcloth; two Sears Roebuck rocking chairs; and a shiny base-burner. That was all the furniture except for a couple of benches and a big oil lamp in the middle of the table. Joey wondered what it must be like not to have a sofa to curl up on.

Mrs. Ryglewicz settled Mom in one of the rockers, and Dad politely sat on a bench. Joey and the twins shared the other bench.

A tiny girl was sitting on a box in the darkest corner, hugging a long rag doll.

"That must be Anna," Joey thought.

"Anna," said Mrs. Ryglewicz, as if in answer to the guess, "bring Papa and Alex. They are working in the garden," she explained, turning to Mom.

"Oh, don't bother them, please," said Mom quickly. "We're only going to be here a short time."

"They will want to see you," Mrs. Ryglewicz said firmly. "Anna!"

The little girl ran out of the room, holding her doll carefully.

"You must have been working very hard to get your home fixed up so nicely in such a short time." Mom looked around with interest. "Did you make the curtains yourself?"

"Yes. I am very fond of sewing. In Poland I was a seamstress. They say I may be able to get work in the clothing factory in Woodville when winter comes and the work here will not be so much.

Mom leaned forward eagerly. "If you're really thinking of taking up sewing professionally again, I hope you'll want to take on some private work. I'm no good with a needle, and I'm in desperate need of some plain dresses and a whole set of draperies. There's never been a seamstress in Cedarville, and it's hopeless trying to get things done by long distance in Atlantic City or Philadelphia."

"I would consider it a great pleasure, but I have no machine."

"I have a sewing machine, and it's been collecting dust since I got it. You could come over and do the work at our house."

"That would be best for fittings and is the way we do it in Poland. I will be glad to come."

"Wonderful!" Mom beamed.

Joey began to twitch. This was like all visits, boring grown-up talk, just the way she'd imagined.

"And here is my husband." Mrs. Ryglewicz smiled at a chunky man in blue overalls who marched through the door with Alex smiling happily behind him.

"And these are the Finches about whom Alex talks, talks, talks all the time. I am delighted to welcome you to my house."

Mr. Ryglewicz stumped briskly around the room, giving everybody's hand a shake. Joey's hand tingled when her turn came, but she smiled back at the twinkle in the funny, creased blue eyes. Donny and Mac, who had evidently been expecting a larger and shyer Alex, looked flabbergasted.

Mr. Ryglewicz soon got settled on the bench beside Dad, with Anna, who had slipped into the room like a tiny rabbit, on his lap.

"Now we will hear all about this wonderful shack that is being built with the help of Alex in the middle of the woods. Whose idea was this?"

"We always build shacks——"

"Vacation and nothing to do——"

"I found Alex in——"

The twins and Joey burst into speech simultaneously.

"Now, now. One at a time and ladies first always."

Mr. Ryglewicz smiled at Joey, who beamed back. He was the nicest grownup she'd ever met. She started her story of finding Alex and getting him to help with the shack, Mac and Donny interrupting every minute and

even Alex throwing in a word or two now and then. Mr.
Ryglewicz listened carefully, giving Anna an occasional
jog when the action went especially fast.

Mom and Dad, who hadn't heard John Rufus's story
about Miss Betsy, were hanging on every word, especially Dad.

"Ghosts, buried treasure, and a mystery," he said
when they finally ran down. "You kids have been having
quite a summer!"

"But there isn't any treasure," said Joey sadly. "That's
just the trouble."

"Bah!" snorted Mr. Ryglewicz. Everybody stared at
him. "You are not looking in the right place, that is all.
Read again this note you have found." The more excited he got, the more peculiar his English became.

"It's gone!" Donny glared at Joey. "This dope lost it."

"I did not!"

"Why not see if with all helping you are not able to
remember? Here is a pencil to write down what the
message was," Mr. Ryglewicz said placidly.

Joey picked up the pencil and screwed up her eyes,
trying to see the faded little note. "I have undertaken
to put a guest on his way to O.P." she wrote slowly.

"'Set,' not 'put,'" said Mac, hanging over her shoulder,
"and I don't think those are the right initials."

"No, stupid. They were D.B. like my first two initials,
Donahue Baird. That's how I remember."

"No fighting until we get home," said Dad rather
grimly.

Joey wisely ignored Donny's insult and made the cor-
rections. "Then what?" she asked.

"Something about the navy," said Mac. "With a funny name."

Joey made a terrible face. "Tar—Tarkiln—no!" There was an intent silence. "Tarshish! Remember the navy of Tarshish!"

"Wow! Good kid!"

"The rest's easy," said Joey offhandedly. "'Key beneath doorstone. Yr. affec. Daughter.' There. We've got it all, but I don't see what good it does us. There aren't any clues that I can see."

"You can't say that until we figure out what it means," objected Mac. "I'd like to know what D.B. stands for, for instance."

"And the navy of Tarshish," said Donny. "That doesn't make any sense at all."

"I may not be a detective," said Mom, "but I know what the navy of Tarshish is. It's in the Bible. The navy that Solomon had."

Mrs. Ryglewicz nodded eagerly. "That is so."

"And we have a Bible, an American Bible," said Mr. Ryglewicz, burrowing behind a curtain that hung over one corner of the room. "Here!"

He handed the Bible to Mom with a bow.

"Now what book is Solomon in?" muttered Mom, flipping the pages rapidly.

"First Kings," said Dad. "I remember that from Sunday School."

Mom found First Kings and began to skim the pages while the children hung over her shoulder eagerly. "Here we are! No. That's the Queen of Sheba. It should be near here—oh!"

"Read it out loud," begged Joey.

"'For the king had at sea a navy of Tarshish with the navy of Hiram: once every three years came the navy of Tarshish bringing gold, and silver, ivory, and apes, and peacocks.'"

"Peacocks!" yelped the twins in unison.

"We must be on the right trail," squealed Joey. "This note must have something to do with the peacock after all."

"Edward Dudley would know what she was talking about," said Dad slowly, "because it was probably a family saying."

"But we still don't know where she hid the peacock," said Donny, "so I don't think we're much further along."

"But this note must tell—in a secret way only Miss Betsy's father would understand. Remember, she thought he was coming back to the Gray Gull. She didn't know he would go straight from Philadelphia to join her in England. That must have been fixed up much later." Mac was running both hands through his hair in his excitement.

"A code, like in Jack Armstrong, the All-American Boy," said Alex proudly. His greatest delight was joining the Finches when they tuned in to radio serials.

"That's the stuff," grinned Joey.

"Good gracious," gasped Mom, looking at her watch. "It's four o'clock. Grandmother will be turning up at any minute. We've got to tear."

"I thought she went home," groaned Donny.

"No, she went over to Atlantic City to pick up some things at Blatt's. Mrs. Ryglewicz, I'm afraid we've stayed much too long, but we've enjoyed our visit so much. I'll come over in a few days to talk some more about the sewing, if I may."

"I shall be pleased."

"And bring Mr. Finch," boomed Mr. Ryglewicz. "I have many questions to ask him about crops."

"Fine," said Dad. "Come on, family." And he herded them briskly out the door and into the car.

"Come over tomorrow," Joey yelled out the window to Alex. He nodded eagerly.

James drove Grandmother in right behind them, and she nodded with approval at everyone's neat appearance.

"I have some things for you, Joanna," she said crisply "Take them up to your room and see what you think of them. If you don't like them, back they go, and your mother will drive you over to Atlantic City to choose new ones."

"Some things" turned out to be two dresses, a jacket, and a pair of neat denim slacks with gay red piping to match the jacket. The dresses were matter-of-fact cottons.

"A sailor dress!" gasped Joey. "Super-duper!"

It was dark blue, with a big flapping collar, a red silk tie, and even a tiny silver anchor swinging jauntily from the tie. Joey decided to wear it to dinner and, after a short struggle with herself, hung up the other dress and put the slacks neatly away.

"How do I look?" she asked Wolf, who only grunted. Joey decided he didn't want her to become a lady.

Grandmother and Mom had more to say on the subject, though, all approving. Even the twins admitted that she looked nice in the sailor dress.

Supper-table conversation was mostly made up of telling Grandmother, who turned out to be unexpectedly interested, about the Ryglewiczes. And from there, the talk swung naturally to the Gray Gull.

Donny, who was in a bad mood because they were having fried clams which he detested, said suddenly, "You know, we don't have any proof that there even was a peacock. The navy of Tarshish could be the British Navy to show her father she was heading for a British warship." He stopped, astonished. "Say, I bet I know what D.B. stands for. Delaware Bay! Sure, that's it! She means she's going to take the ensign to the Bay shore, and if her father wants to follow her she'll be with the English Navy."

Mac, easily persuaded by Donny as usual, said, "We don't even know there was a Captain Bones, let alone a peacock. That's all a legend, maybe."

Joey was about to launch into battle when help came from a most unexpected ally.

"Nonsense," said Grandmother, much as Mr. Ryglewicz had said "Bah!" that afternoon. "Of course there was a Captain Bones. My great-great-grandfather knew him personally."

Everybody's mouth dropped open, Dad's widest of all.

"What do you mean, Grandmother?" asked Joey weakly.

"Just what I said," snapped Grandmother. "I come from an old South Jersey family, and until the War of 1812 my mother's ancestors lived in Cape May County, not far from here, as a matter of fact."

"Why didn't you tell us before?" groaned Mac.

"Because nobody asked me. None of my family has ever shown anything but distressed boredom when I mention my ancestry—you especially, Frederic—and I certainly was not aware that you were chasing the history of the Gray Gull." Grandmother paused dramatically and dropped her bombshell. "Edward Dudley was my mother's great-great-uncle."

Dad put his hand to his head as if to hold it on. "You mean we are descended from the family who came down and tried to run the inn in John Rufus's story?"

"That was another branch of the family. My mother's connection was through a sister of Edward Dudley. Eventually, however, when the Dudleys left the Gray Gull for good and all, several trunkloads of their possessions found their way to my grandmother's attic, for want of anything better to do with them. I believe I turned them over to you and Louise, in case you wanted to lend them to the county museum."

Mom shook her head. "That was the winter you had flu and had to go to Florida, Mother. We got the trunks all right but no message as to what to do with them, so I assumed they were clothes for the children's dressing-up games. They're still in the attic."

"So that's how we got Miss Betsy's riding cape," cried Joey triumphantly.

"And we have a right to the peacock, if we find it!" finished Mac.

14
A Cranberry Fight

JOEY could hardly wait for breakfast to be over next morning so that she could start everyone for the Glade. But just as she pushed back her chair Dad threw a spanner in the works.

"Picking starts today," he announced, "and we'll need all hands—Donny and Mac for picking, Joey and Mom for sorting."

Joey started to whine and then thought better of it. No argument would be any use against the urgency of getting in the berries before frost could strike. No one would ever forget the year they had frost in August and lost the whole crop. Least of all Dad.

Dew was still glistening on the vetch in the field beside the house as she and Mom started to walk up to the packing house. Joey looked at the goldenrod and Queen Anne's lace and shuddered. "School soon."

"Mom," she burst out, "if you and Dad liked Holly River so much that you chose it as the place you wanted to live in, why do you want to send us away to Philadelphia?"

Mom stopped walking and put her hand on Joey's shoulder. "Dad and I don't ever want to send you away from us, Joey. You must never think that. But there are so many things that people need when they're growing up, the kind of things Holly River doesn't have—good schools, good friends and plenty of them, and the chance to learn how other people live."

"Then if you don't want to send us away, I guess you won't," Joey said hopefully.

Mom's hand tightened on her shoulder. "It's very hard to explain. Remember when Wolf had worms and you let him go to the vet's to be treated? You knew you'd miss Wolf, but you wanted him to go and get well. Do you see what I mean?"

"I guess so," said Joey, "though I wish Grandmother would let us alone."

"Yes." Mom's face took on the anxious look that meant she was thinking about Grandmother and Philadelphia.

But it was hard to be worried really, in the cedary wind, with sand crunching underfoot warmly, Wolf ki-yi-ing after a rabbit, and the sweet voices of the pickers floating up from the Brook Bog.

The women who were going to sort the cranberries for packing were waiting in front of the packing house. They were divided into two camps—the wives of the pickers who could be spared now for this work; and the locals from Cedarville, who came out annually for the sorting and considered the others "foreigners." Mom, who was boss of the sorting, threatened every year to fire one group or the other because of the trouble the hard feelings caused, but neither could ever be spared.

The inside of the packing house, dark and cool with its blank walls and concrete floor, was a beehive of activity.

Boxes of berries were already pouring in from the

bogs, where the pickers had been working since five. John Rufus, who bossed the packing while Dad supervised the picking, was directing a gang of men who wheeled the boxes on giant wheelbarrows into the big open elevator, hauled by hand, where they were carried to the second floor. Joey was terrified of the elevator.

"Come on, girls," called Mom, with her pleasant smile. The women liked her, even if they disliked all their fellow workers.

"Good crop this year, Miz Finch?" asked Mrs. Smith, Vangie's mother. She stumped up the ladder-like wood stairs right after Mom.

"Fair, I think." Mom unlocked the door of the sorting room. "I'll assign the chairs and then we can start."

The sorting room was large, with windows all around the three walls. Under the windows were tables with little wooden walls around the edges to keep the berries from bouncing out. Under Mom's brisk orders the women were soon seated at the tables, and Mom turned to John Rufus, who was standing in the doorway.

"You can start the berries moving down here, John Rufus. We're all set."

He vanished, and in a few minutes there was a low rumble in the chutes, hanging above the tables like wooden mail chutes. Berries began bouncing down on the tables, to be scooped to one side and sorted by practiced fingers. Good berries were shoved into one hole in the table, bad berries into another. The holes opened into more chutes that carried the good berries down to the packing room on the first floor, the bad berries to dumps outside. The only sound was the rattle of the cranberries. Mom was firm about not talking.

Joey saw that Mom was busy instructing a new girl and slipped quickly out the door before Mom could put her to work, sorting. She wandered up to the third floor, where the men were dumping boxes of unsorted berries into the big boxlike contraption that fed the chutes into the sorting room.

"Want a ride on the elevator, Jo'nna?" Horace Smith, Vangie's brother, was leering at her. He was a great big hulking fellow who was still in eighth grade though he was nearly sixteen. Joey knew he was mean enough to take her on the elevator willy-nilly, just because he knew she was scared of it.

"Not me!" she called above the din, and ducked quickly down the stairs.

There was more doing on the first floor.

"Joanna, you get out of here," yelled John Rufus, after one of the men nearly upset a flat truck, loaded with trays of cranberries, trying to avoid running her down.

A few skips and she was safely hidden in a corner with a few spiders for company. "Wish I'd brought a book," Joey thought sleepily. "It's too nice a day for working."

"Psst!" She jumped off her board seat and looked wildly around. "Psst! Over here!"

Five heads rose slowly from behind a pile of empty trays: two yellow, one red, one tan, and one black.

"Well, I'll be!" said Joey. "How did you get here?"

"Easy!" said Baptista. "Mac and Donny and I just picked berries farther and farther away from the other pickers until we sneaked into the woods at the edge of the bog and got clean away. It's not the kind of day for working, we decided."

"I decided that too!" Joey was struck by the coincidence.

"I found them sneaking through the woods," said Ted.

"And I came from the house where the good grandmother told me you were in the packing house," Alex added proudly.

Joey giggled loudly at the thought of the "good grandmother" and was told to shut up.

"What shall we do?" asked Mac, wriggling to the top of the trays. "How about playing King of the Mountain? I'm King."

"Too noisy," Donny said briefly.

"Ride in the big wheelbarrow," suggested Ted.

The others looked at him admiringly.

"Great!" said Mac.

"There's Horace bringing down a load of empty boxes on the big wheelbarrow now," whispered Joey, peering from her vantage point. "You go over and start teasing him, Donny. While he's chasing you, we'll grab the barrow."

"Suppose he catches me," complained Donny. "He'll beat me to a pulp."

"He won't, scaredy. You can run about three times as fast as he can, the big lump. Go on!"

"Well, okay."

Donny darted off, and a few minutes later they saw him talking to Horace. The big fat face got redder and redder, and finally he bellowed like a mad buck, and lunged at Donny, only to grab empty air. Donny had ducked and was dodging neatly in and out of the piles of trays with Horace lumbering in pursuit.

They vanished, and Joey gestured wildly. "Come on!"

By the time Donny panted back, the wheelbarrow was a cannon-ball express, wheeling Joey, Baptista, and Alex, with Ted and Mac pushing it.

"Eeee!" squealed Baptista, covering her eyes as they sped around a sharp corner.

"All right now. You kids are going to get a good licking if you're not out of here by the time I count ten."

John Rufus shook his fist at them ferociously as the express rounded a pile of boards and stopped practically on his toes. The Finches knew when they had gone too far. In two minutes the packing house was cleared of children.

"Gosh!" Mac threw himself down on the grass. "Doesn't look as if we'll have any fun today. Maybe we'd better give up and go back to picking."

Joey stared hopefully around. They were under the sorting-room windows, and the chutes down which the rotten berries were tossed opened out of the wall above them. Already a large pile of berries had grown beneath each chute. Joey had one of her splendid ideas.

"Let's have a rotten-berry fight," she said.

The boys caught fire immediately. "We can divide into

two teams and each take a heap for a fort, like we do
with snow," said Donny.

"Neat!" Mac scrambled up and headed for a pile. "I
choose Ted!"

Baptista looked distastefully at the rapidly darkening berries. "I think I'd better go pick," she announced.

"Oh no!" cried Joey. "You'll love this game."

"Sure. Stay, Baptista. You can be on my team." Mac looked at her wheedlingly.

"Wel-l-l," Baptista gave Carmencita's carriage a thoughtful jog. "I guess so."

She walked slowly over to Mac and Ted. The other three leaped for the remaining pile and began burrowing from the top down, to make themselves a wall. Unlike snow, cranberries roll, and making a wall proved to be difficult. The steady rain of berries from the chute didn't help either, but finally Donny decided they were ready.

"I declare war!" he shouted, putting his head over the barricade.

"Ready, aim, FIRE!" came Mac's voice from the enemy fort, and a fusillade of berries hit him in the head.

The berries made perfect weapons. When thrown hard enough they really stung, but most of the time they merely spattered, so each aim was a challenge. Joey burrowed and threw, burrowed and threw, and got so good that she had the satisfaction of seeing the enemy faces become redder and juicier with each throw. Baptista had no pitching arm whatsoever, and Mac's aim was wild, so Ted's skill was helpless against the barrage from Donny's team. Even Alex made up for his wild aim by being twice as fast as anyone else, and before long Donny whispered, "We'll storm them now. Ready?"

Alex and Joey nodded.

"Then, CHARGE!"

"Ah-uh-ah-uh-ah!" shrieked Joey in a truly terrifying imitation of Tarzan, tumbling after him.

Her battle cry had the wrong effect, though, because it frightened Alex, who forgot to charge and simply stood quaking in the deserted fort. He stared after the brave attackers for a minute as they scrambled toward the other fort, scooping up falling berries and hurling them as they ran. Then he caught on.

"Jack Armstrong, the Al-l-l American Boy!" he whooped, and charged into the fray.

Nobody noticed when the windows of the sorting room flew open.

Joey felt as if she was skating on a sea of cranberries; they rolled and split and popped under her feet so that she lost a step for nearly every one she gained. And the firing from the enemy was much more deadly now that the targets were at close range. The air was full of cranberries, and it became hard to open her eyes long enough to take aim. Then suddenly, miraculously, the berries stopped. Joey opened her eyes and looked into three stricken faces.

"Joanna," said a cool voice. "Mackenzie. Donahue. Come here."

Joey swung slowly around. Mom was standing in the door of the packing house.

15

Ted to the Rescue

"It's been decided." Mac's face looked green in the dusky light as he crouched on the floor of Joey's room.

Donny and Joey looked away. They knew they didn't want to hear what he was going to say.

"Dad almost caught me once, but I managed to hear most of it. Lucky it's still warm enough for them to sit on the porch. That roof wasn't so hot, though. I thought I was going to fall a couple of times."

"And Mac's trying to put off saying it," Joey thought, "because then it will be true."

"Go on," muttered Donny.

"You and I aren't going to Philadelphia at all. We're going to Lawrenceville. Grandmother knows the headmaster, so it isn't too late to get us in."

"That's not bad at all. I bet they have a neat football team. And with two of us it shouldn't be too rough."

Joey felt an awful clotting in her throat. "What about me?" she whispered.

It was Mac's turn to look away. "You're going to live with Grandmother and go to a girls' school near her house."

"I'm sorry, Joey." Sympathy from Donny was more

than Joey could stand. The tears began trickling down
her nose.

All alone in Grandmother's house without even the
twins for company.

Finally Mac began crawling toward the door. "We
better get going before somebody comes up. Don't take
it too hard, Joey. You can probably come home for
Christmas and stuff."

The minute the door clicked softly closed, Joey
climbed on her bed and buried her head in the pillow.
She cried harder than she ever had in her life. The bed
shook so hard with her sobs that she was afraid Mom
would hear and come up, so she sat up and managed to
stop crying by thinking hard about John Rufus's story
about Miss Betsy Dudley.

"She was brave and I can be too," she whispered
bracingly.

And then the thought came, "She ran away and so
will I!"

She scrambled off the bed and began to dress. Dungarees, sneakers, jersey, plaid shirt because late summer
nights were chilly. After a moment's thought, she dug
around in a drawer until she found her spare toothbrush,
a comb, and her sheath knife. And because she might
want something to read, she grabbed *The Five Little
Peppers* off the bookshelf. She tied everything up in a
bandanna, and took a last look around. It was hard to
leave, but anything was better than going to live with
Grandmother.

The climb from window to roof to grape arbor had
never seemed easier. Joey was down in a trice. As she
paused by the back door, Wolf rose like a gray shadow

in the twilight and padded to her heels. Joey wanted to hug him. At least she wouldn't be alone.

Grown-up voices still sounded from the porch, so she was safe from detection. She turned and walked silently down the driveway and off toward the Brook Bog dam.

Although it was only twilight the woods seemed really dark. And full of noises. Joey held onto Wolf's collar for comfort, but the farther she went into the trees, the harder it was to force each foot forward. Miss Betsy, she remembered shakily, had at least had her midshipman for company—and protection. Suppose Captain Bones appeared in front of her, demanding his peacock. Or she saw the red light of Uncle Tom-Tom's hanting eye coming toward her down the path.

"I'm Princess Snow Flower, the fearless Indian maiden," she whispered through chattering teeth. But it didn't help much to pretend. Even the pretending scared her.

A twig snapped under one foot and she jumped. Far off in the woods a whippoorwill started to chant sadly. Joey plowed doggedly on. Shadows grew into shapes, shapes grew bigger and started to move. Her legs were shaking now.

"Whish!" A ghostly hand swept across her face.

"It's only a branch," said Joey's mind. But her legs gave up. They let her down on the trail, and she sat there, too frightened to move, too frightened to stay still.

"I guess I'd rather live with Grandmother," moaned Joey, and burst into tears.

Wolf snuggled against her, trying to figure out what the trouble was.

"Joey," said a voice in the darkness right over her head.

Joey felt that her heart had stopped completely. She flung both arms around Wolf and buried her head in his neck.

"It's me. Ted," the voice said comfortingly.

Joey jumped up. The shapes receded. Trees and bushes were trees and bushes again.

"Gee, am I glad to see you," she sighed.

"What are you doing out here?"

"I was running away." Her voice cracked in a humiliating sob.

"Crying? Why?"

"Be-because I'm so scared. I keep thinking Uncle Tom-Tom will come along and get me."

Ted looked up at the trees as if ideas grew on branches. "Family looking for you?"

"No. They never check once I'm in bed."

"Then come and see Uncle Tom-Tom."

"What?" Joey turned as if to head for home.

Ted put his hand firmly on her shoulder. "Never get over being scared if you don't. He's my uncle. Everybody's uncle where I live. He likes those stories about him because he doesn't want to be bothered with a lot of outsiders. But he's really kind. You'll like him."

"Well, at least I've heard you say more than four words at one time," said Joey shakily. "If you can do that, I guess I can go see Uncle Tom-Tom. But you've got to promise to stick to me like a burr."

"Right." Ted wheeled and led the way into the woods.

Joey tightened her hold on Wolf's collar and followed him.

The trek through the woods was like a dream. Joey soon gave up any idea of keeping her bearings. She fol-

lowed Ted blindly, and soon the squish of wet ground
and the spring of long moss under her feet told her that
they were in a swamp. They made their way more slowly
now, often teetering over fallen logs or crawling on hands
and knees through a big briar patch. Joey felt, without
knowing why, that the deeper they went, the older the
swamp became. There were fewer briars, bigger trees,
and the darkness became deeper and more silent. She
began to have the feeling that a dinosaur out of Mac's
prehistoric animals book might come lumbering at them
through the trees.

Then, just as suddenly, they were on dry ground.

"We're nearly there," whispered Ted softly. "This is
like your place—an island in swampland. Uncle Tom-
Tom's shack is over there."

Sure enough, a little light glowed through the oaks
and cedars. Joey's heart began to pound.

There was nothing frightening about the little house.
Like most of the homes in the county it was unpainted,
but, as it had been built of good cedar slabs, it had
weathered to a pretty silver instead of a ramshackle gray.
It was small and square and had a window on each side
of the front door. A big wisteria vine was draped over
one side of the house, and a magnolia tree stood guard
in front.

Ted stepped up to the door and rapped quietly. Three
times.

"It's Ted," he said clearly.

There was a sound of movement in the house and then
the door began to swing slowly open. Joey dug her
fingers into the long fur at Wolf's neck. What was behind
that door? She had to force herself to look.

Then the door was open, and a tiny figure stood in the light from the kerosene lamp.

"Glad to see you, boy," said a cracked voice.

Joey knew that Uncle Tom-Tom must be very, very, old. He was no taller than she was and bent as a pine knot. But his skin was brown, and he moved as briskly as a young man.

"Come in and bring your friend." They were waved in through the door.

And such a cozy room met Joey. A sofa with great comfortable sags, guns and traps hung handily on the wall, an old potbellied stove, a well-padded rocking chair.

"Who's the little lady?" Uncle Tom-Tom turned from

closing the door, and Joey screwed up all her courage
and looked at his eyes.

They sparkled all right, but they were blue, not red,
and he had two of them. Joey heaved a great sigh of
relief.

"I'm Joanna Finch," she said shyly. "I live over at
Holly River."

"That's right. Your dad's that crazy feller trying to
raise cranberries. Come and set."

Joey curled up in one of the sofa sags, and Ted made
himself comfortable in the other.

"Been hunting for Captain Bones's peacock, have
you?" Uncle Tom-Tom's face was as sly as an old
possum's.

"How did you know?" Joey sat up in surprise.

"Know everything that goes on in these woods and swamps. Get discouraged yet?"

"A little," Joey admitted. "Do you know anything about the treasure, Uncle Tom-Tom?"

The old man winked. "I might. But you'll have to do the finding. Be bad luck if a Dudley didn't turn up the bird."

"But I'm not a Dudley."

"You'll do for one. Your Grandmother's related to the Dudleys."

Was there anything Uncle Tom-Tom didn't know? Ted's eyes were sparkling too. "It's still there?"

"That's for me to know and you to find out." Uncle Tom-Tom cackled slyly. "But I'll tell you one thing. Not many folks around here are going to risk fooling with Bones's ghost to find out."

"You mean there is a ghost." The hair on Joey's neck began to crawl.

"No more than I have an evil eye. But most everybody believes in both of them."

"Uncle Tom-Tom," asked Joey, "why *do* people in Cedarville think you have a red hanting eye?"

Uncle Tom-Tom's face began to look like John Rufus's did when he was about to start one of his tales. As if he were seeing something far, far away. "When I was a sight younger than I am now," he said, "I decided I wanted to see what lay beyond the swamps. In those days, we didn't even go outside to school, like Ted here does. So I walked into Cedarville to have a look around. The Cedarvillers were scared to death of us Pineys (mainly because they'd hardly even laid eyes on one of us), and when I came walking up the street the women called their children in the houses and locked the doors.

"But one little girl didn't run away. Too little to be afraid. She came right up to me and I gave her a pat on the head. Then I went back home and never left the swamps again, because I hadn't liked what I saw of the outside. But that little girl died of the summer sickness three weeks later, and the stories started going around that I'd put a hant on her. And the stories got bigger and bigger with each telling, so that in ten years time I had a red eye and all the rest of it."

Uncle Tom-Tom's eyes came back to Joey again. "That's the only thing you've ever got to be afraid of, Jo'nna. Believing what's not true. You can shoot a bear, but you can't fight the fear that lying tongues put in your own mind."

And at long last Joey knew why Mom and Dad and Grandmother hated superstition and why they would rather have her live in Philadelphia than have her believe as the Cedarvillers did.

"I'd better get you home," said Ted matter-of-factly. "Don't want your dad out looking for you with the state police."

"That's right." Uncle Tom-Tom hopped up to open the door. "Good-by, Jo'nna. Come and see me again."

"I will," Joey promised gladly.

There was nothing frightening about the swamps on the way home. Joey walked quietly along, thinking of what Uncle Tom-Tom had said.

"Maybe being afraid of going to live with Grandmother is like being afraid of ghosts," she thought.

"There might not be anything bad about it when you came right down to doing it."

"Here you are." Ted stopped, and Joey saw that they were behind the grape arbor. "Want a hand up?"

"You know everything—just like Uncle Tom-Tom." Joey giggled. "Even how I sneak in and out of my room. Good night and thank you for taking me there."

But Ted had already vanished.

16

Joey Finds the Treasure

THE next week wasn't as bad as it might have been. Grandmother went off to Philadelphia to see about getting the twins admitted to Lawrenceville and Joey to the school near her home. The Finches settled down to work, the boys picking and Joey sorting. She was quite a good sorter when she put her mind to it, and she had to concentrate on the berries all the time, so her brain wasn't free to worry about the fall. But it was dreadful not to be able to get to the Glade.

The twins seemed to have lost interest in Captain Bones's peacock again, but Joey studied the message they had written out at the Ryglewicz' whenever she had a spare minute. Before long she had it memorized, so she no longer had to look at the paper. But she still couldn't make any clues out.

"Thank goodness," Mom said late one afternoon. "That was the last box."

Dad looked thoughtfully around the sorting room. He had dropped in to see how things were going. "The freight car picks up the boxes at the railroad siding at Cedarville tomorrow morning. We're through for another year.

"Right now I'm going home and sleep for a week—
as soon as I pay off the sorters, of course."

"John Rufus will pay them with the men," Dad said.
He got what Mom called his "guilty smile" on his face.
"Can you put off that sleep for a bit, Louise? Mother
is on her way down, and I'm expecting another visitor
tonight. I meant to tell you but it slipped my mind."

"You!" Mom ran her hands through her hair the way
Mac did. "All right. Who is it?"

"A former professor of mine. John Applegate. I
worked with him when I was getting my graduate
degree in history."

"I remember. He wanted you to go on and get your
Ph.D. and go into teaching and research. He even
offered you a job." She pinched Dad's nose. "Only you'd
met me and seen Holly River."

"Want me to run ahead and tell Beulah to make up
the beds in Donny's room and the spare room?" asked
Joey.

Mom looked impressed. "I don't know what I'll do
without you this winter, Joey. Yes, please do."

Mac and Donny were doing a war dance on the lawn
to celebrate the end of picking when Joey arrived.
Carmencita was in the center like a white captive, and
Baptista was watching admiringly from the sidelines.

"Was there ever worse luck than we have?" moaned
Joey as she trotted up.

The war dance stopped abruptly.

"Grandmother and an old school teacher arriving at
the same time. I can't stand it."

From the groans, neither could Mac and Donny.

"Stay the night, Baptista," Joey begged. "That will

help some, and you'll be leaving tomorrow, remember, and I won't see you till next summer."

"You'll see me in Philadelphia," Baptista said practically.

"That's true." Joey brightened at this reminder of the one cheerful spot in the winter's plans. "But spend the night anyway. Coax your mother."

"All right. I'll take Carmencita home and ask her right now."

"You'd better go help Beulah move your things into Mac's room," Joey told Donny.

"Yeah." He wandered off with startling good nature. Since Joey's sentence of doom both twins had been unnaturally pleasant to her.

Professor Applegate and Grandmother arrived at the same time—together, in fact, for Grandmother had offered the Professor a ride from Philadelphia in her car. He wasn't at all like a teacher. He was tall and thin and white-haired and never heard anything. Joey decided he was deaf, because every remark had to be repeated at least twice, before he would look up and say, "Uh-ah, what was that?"

They waited for Grandmother to lecture him for not paying attention, but she just repeated everything patiently.

Baptista came back with her toothbrush and nightgown and permission to spend the night. She was just in time for supper, which was one of Mom's super meals. The Professor had two helpings of everything.

The apple pie was being passed when he said, right in the middle of Grandmother's story about what she had said to the headmaster of Lawrenceville, "Tell me about the buried treasure."

Grandmother began to glare and then quickly changed the glare into a polite smile.

Joey looked over at the twins. Everyone had heard about the peacock, it seemed. She wasn't sure she liked the idea.

"How did you know about the treasure, sir?" she asked politely.

"Uh-ah, what was that?"

"How did you hear about the treasure? We thought it was a secret."

"Quite. Your father told me. In the strictest confidence, of course." The Professor smiled, and Joey knew he could be trusted.

Once again she and the boys told the story, with Baptista to help out this time.

"Most ingenious work," said the Professor when they had finished. "Eh, Finch? I know a great many men who would give up their degrees just to find out half of what you've told me. This part of the country is a great mystery to historians. The people are close. Keep their stories to themselves."

"But Dad has a lot of dia——" Joey stopped short at Dad's ferocious frown. Luckily the Professor didn't seem to have heard her.

After dinner, the talk was about schoolish things, and very boring. Joey was relieved when Mom sent her and Baptista off to bed.

Once in bed she had a hard time getting to sleep, though. Baptista dropped off immediately, but Joey had her mind on Miss Betsy and a lot of other things.

When she finally dozed off she thought she hadn't really gone to sleep. The room was full of moonlight, and it got lighter and lighter until a pretty lady came stepping through the window. She was slim and dark and wore a gray dress with a red cape over it. Joey knew it was Miss Betsy.

"Where did I hide the key?" Miss Betsy's voice was the sweetest thing Joey had ever heard.

"Under the doorstep," she answered calmly.

"Ah, but that's not where the *key* goes. You heard the story."

"The peacock!" Joey shouted, and at the loud noise, Miss Betsy vanished. Joey sat up in bed and realized that she had dreamed the whole thing. Baptista was sleeping peacefully beside her.

"What a crazy dream," she chuckled. "I'm glad I've finally seen Miss Betsy!"

She flopped down on the pillow again and let the dream drift drowsily through her mind. And suddenly it came to her! She sat bolt upright.

"John Rufus's grandfather said they always hung the key inside the stable door! And Edward Dudley would know that. Then why did Miss Betsy tell her father in a note that the key was in the wrong place when she was in a tearing hurry to get the midshipman away to the Delaware Bay?"

The answer was as plain as the snub nose on Joey's face. Careful not to wake Baptista, she hurried out of bed and yanked on some clothes. She had to find out if her hunch was right.

There was no moon and the low clouds hid the stars. Joey was glad she had thought to bring a flashlight. She

trotted down the road toward the Glade, Wolf padding
at her heels. The woods rustled darkly, but now they
were friendly and familiar sounds—the cheep of a bird
wakened by her light, the crackle of a small animal
going about its business, the gentle sigh of the breeze.

"It's nice not to be afraid any more, isn't it?" Joey
said to Wolf. He agreed silently.

It was also nice to see the Glade again, after being
away for such a long time. Even the shack looked quite
handsome in the light of her flashlight, its defects hidden in the darkness.

"Now let's see." Joey shone her light along the line of
half-excavated bricks. "This should be the front wall,
the way we figured it. And the front door would have
been somewhere along it."

She got down on her hands and knees and began to
dig methodically along the rough line, searching for
the large flatness of a flagstone. Smart Miss Betsy, to
choose such an obvious place for her treasure. Who
would think to look under his own front step?

"Gosh," she muttered after a few minutes, "I wish you
could hold the light, Wolf. I can't dig and hold it at
the same time."

She rested on her heels and tried to figure out a way
both to see and work. For the first time she was sorry
she hadn't got Baptista up and made her come too.

"But then it wouldn't be my discovery, and if I was
wrong I'd sure get laughed at. There must be a way to
do it alone."

Joey tried tucking the flashlight under her chin, but
it kept rolling out every time she moved. Finally she
hit upon laying it on the ground beside her, and al-

though it wasn't a perfect system the light was fairly good when she propped up the handle on a brick.

"Whew," she sighed at last, "this wall must be a mile long. Funny how much quicker it went with six of us working. It's going to be daylight before I finish, at this rate."

Wolf had been watching her earnestly, his eyes green in the reflected light. Now he advanced to her side and began to dig furiously, his paws going like pistons.

Joey laughed. "Good boy!" She gave him a hard pat. "You *can* help, can't you?"

The digging went faster with Wolf's help, but sometimes he was more of a hindrance, for he kept getting off the track and covering Joey's excavations with flying dirt. Then she would have to stop and start him in the right place again.

"And stop knocking over the flashlight," she pleaded, after he had done it for the fifth time. "Oh dear! Is that sunrise over there?"

It wasn't, but it seemed as if, with every minute, an hour of the night went by.

Wolf had been snuffling wildly, and suddenly he put his nose to the ground, his tail whirling like a windmill, and started off on a trail.

"Wolf, come back!" Joey shouted. She was nearly ready to quit and go home for help.

But Wolf was too excited to pay any attention. He slammed to a halt by a rabbit hole and began to dig frantically.

"Pest!" Joey got stiffly to her feet and marched over to him. She grabbed his collar and started to haul him away. This was certainly the last straw.

"Ugh! Stop that awful scratching with your toe nails. Come on, silly dog. You'll never get to that rabbit through solid rock."

Wolf seemed to think he would. Finally Joey got down beside him for a good tug. She saw what he was unearthing.

"Oh, Wolf," she gasped. "I think you've found it!"

She shoved Wolf to one side in her excitement. The stone was indeed large and flat; the more of it she uncovered, the more it looked like a flagstone. Joey suddenly discovered she didn't want to go on. Suppose the peacock wasn't there and another awful disappointment was waiting for her? Her hands slowed. But she had to know. With a sigh she put her hands under the barely uncovered stone and heaved.

"Drat! I'm not strong enough. Wolf, how did John Rufus get that oak stump out of the backyard? No, he didn't use a block and tackle. You'll have to think better

than that. It was a—a crowbar! He pried it out with a
crowbar. Help me find a big strong stick."

But Wolf thought it would be more fun to find a big
strong rabbit, so Joey had to hunt her own stick. She
managed, with many grunts and groans, to root out a
small sapling that looked as if it might do the trick.

"I couldn't do this if I wasn't so excited," Joey panted.
"Come on, Wolf, help me dig out under the stone."

Wolf was perfectly willing to help with the digging,
and they soon had a hole big enough to get one end of
the sapling into it. Joey stood up and grabbed the other
end firmly. Then she leaned down on it with all her
might. The stone began to wobble. Wolf barked fren-
ziedly. Joey leaned again—and again. The stone rose
slowly, with a shower of sand and leaves like a minia-
ture earthquake. Joey pushed her lever forward and it
toppled over on its back.

Joey knelt by the hole. She was afraid to look.

Wolf turned toward the edge of the clearing and
began to growl ominously.

"Be quiet!" Joey snapped impatiently. But the growls
rumbled into a ferocious barking. Joey suddenly realized
that there seemed to be a whole herd of cows crashing
through the woods toward them.

"I don't care if it's wild bears coming to eat me up,"
she muttered. "I've got to see if anything's in that hole."
And she shined her flashlight downward. The light
bounced up from a smooth surface of black metal!

"Joey! Joey, where are you?" Mom's voice echoed
lonesomely around the clearing and was picked up by a
whole chorus. "Joey!"

She turned around reluctantly. The whole family was

parading across the clearing, looking like a piece out of
the circus. Mac and Donny were the clowns in flapping
polka-dot pajamas. Then Baptista, a dainty fairy in her
soft white nightie, an illusion that ended at her feet with
Joey's old red bunny slippers. Mom was the fat lady in
a great flannel bathrobe of Dad's, and he was a sort of
upside-down ringmaster with a striped blazer over his
white pajamas. Over his shoulder bounced a great white
cabbage that turned out to be Grandmother's head in an
immense ruffled nightcap. But Professor Applegate was
the star turn, for he was wrapped in Mom's best pink
silk bedspread, and rustled along like a tall, thin ghost
at Grandmother's side.

Joey didn't stop to wonder what they were all doing
there. "I've found it!" she screamed. "Come and look!"

The next half hour was like another dream. Mac and
Dad hauling up the thing at the bottom of the hole that
turned out to be a small and very rusty iron box. Joey
and Baptista dancing around them like a couple of crazy
imps. Grandmother saying every five minutes, "I wonder
what these children will find to do next," and Professor
Applegate muttering right after her, "Bless my soul.
Early eighteenth-century ironwork. Remarkable!"

Mom finally managed to restore order by calling
firmly, "Cocoa and apple pie at home!"

"Yes," said Dad in a dazed voice, "it's no use trying to
open this thing here. I'll have to get a chisel. Here,
Donny, let me carry it."

And back they marched, with Joey in the middle like
a conquering hero.

Nobody wanted to wait for the cocoa before trying to

open the box, but Mom was adamant. "We all need nourishment," she said.

The Professor was the first to side with her. "We must be careful opening the box," he said. "Very careful. Imagine the slightest damage to the contents!"

Joey shuddered and hurried to the kitchen after Baptista, who was already busy helping Mom lay out cups and plates.

When they got back to the living room, each carrying a tray, Dad was helping the Professor to rummage in Mom's desk.

"What in the world?" asked Mom.

"Keys," said Dad busily. "We're looking for keys. And that oil you use for your sewing machine. Professor Applegate thinks we may be able to unlock the box."

He was staring down at three nail files, a Christmas-tree bulb, two combs, and six large screws. "Where are the keys, Louise?" he asked helplessly.

Mom blushed and looked sideways at Grandmother. Joey knew Grandmother didn't approve of the way Mom kept a handy assortment of supplies in her desk. The desk had belonged to Grandmother's mother and, to her mind, was a place for letters and stamps only. But as Mom pointed out, the desk was central and there was nothing like pigeon holes for storing string and screw drivers.

"You're looking in the wrong place." Mom flipped open a tiny drawer and hauled out a great chain of keys and a little can of oil. "Here they are."

Grandmother frowned. "I've left some keys on my dresser," she remembered. "Joanna, run up and get them."

Joey stared at the little iron box, sitting rather grubbily in the middle of the coffee table.

"I don't think we ought to open it tonight," she said reluctantly.

Mac and Donny set up a howl, but Baptista looked at her fondly. "Alex and Ted," she said softly.

"That's right. After all, they were just as anxious to find the treasure as we were, and they helped a lot. It would be cheating them to open it when they're not here."

"Be quiet, boys," said Dad sharply. "Joey found the box, and if she wants to open it tomorrow, that's what we'll do. Everybody eat up and then get to bed."

The twins started to sulk, but they couldn't resist the sight of Mom's pie and in a minute were gobbling it up.

"Up you go," said Mom, as Baptista and Joey polished the last of the forks with their towels.

"I won't be able to sleep," Joey sighed. She had been regretting her decision to hold off on the box opening.

"It's just like Christmas Eve," Baptista said wisely. "You never think you're going to sleep, and the next thing you know it's morning."

And she turned out to be absolutely right.

17
Holly River Secret

"I GUESS I'd better ride my bike over to get Alex," Donny said at breakfast.

"It's too far," Mac objected. "The only short way is to cut through the state forest, and the roads are too soft for a bike."

"Not after the frost," said Donny triumphantly. "We had one early this morning. Good thing we got the berries picked."

Joey rushed to the window. Sure enough, the ground was still trimmed with a delicate white sprinkling.

"Wow! It was early this year."

Dad cleared his throat. "I'll run you over in the car. The Professor wants to have a look at our county, and that will give me a good chance to show him around without walking."

The children grinned. Dad was clearly as anxious as they were to get the unveiling under way.

"And Baptista and I will take a walk and see if we pick up Ted going through the woods." Joey rushed for the kitchen, balancing a stack of dishes a foot high. She could hear Grandmother explaining to the Professor that the children usually had better manners than to clear and stack at the table.

"I like this weather." Baptista pranced along, as gay and chipper as a robin in Joey's red cardigan.

"Me too. But I wish we'd find old Ted. We've been gone an awful long time."

"Where are we?"

"Nearly to the Deer Head. We passed the Holly Swamp a good way back. Did you notice it?"

"I thought it looked kind of familiar, but woods and swamps all look the same to me still," Baptista confessed.

"You'll learn next summer. We'll go for more hikes then. We'll be too old for dolls."

"But not for plays. Maybe we can finish the Cinderella costumes and put on the play."

Joey still felt a little guilty about the way she had dropped the Cinderella project. Still, they couldn't have done both, and finding the treasure was much more important, any way you looked at it.

"I'm glad Pop decided to come back next year. He says it's good for us to spend the summer in the country, and it's much better here than at the peach orchards."

Joey looked at Baptista admiringly. Baptista never held grudges, and she was certainly a good sport. It seemed you could be pretty and dainty and still be a good sport. Joey decided she would try to learn how to do that herself. This winter would be a perfect time.

"We'll play dolls all summer if you want," she said generously.

Baptista giggled. "Oh no, Joey! You'd never be happy doing that. We'll take walks and things too. Maybe we'll even build our own shack."

Joey walked on, dreaming of the splendid shack they would have as a playhouse.

"Is this another cranberry bog?" Baptista's timid voice roused her, and she looked around rather wildly.

"We've got to the Deer Head. Those boys will have our heads, we'll be so late getting back. Come on. We'd better run."

"Look!" Baptista's voice was no more than a whisper. She hung on to Joey's sleeve and pointed.

The frost had swept the vines a deep red, and, with the same cool brush, had wiped away all traces of the man-scent, left by the pickers. Now the sun made the bog a warm, inviting playground. A deer stepped out from the bright maples and dark oaks across the bog and pranced delicately toward the center. A line of fawn shadows followed, their heads tossed warily to the breeze.

"They look as if they're doing a dance," breathed Baptista, and Joey nodded.

Then the spell was snapped. A boy stepped through the trees at the head of the bog. A flicker of slender necks and legs and the deer were gone. Joey wanted to cry.

"It's Ted," Baptista said crossly. "The mean thing frightened those darling deer. What were they doing?"

"Playing. Dad used to see them often when he first moved to Holly River, but they don't often come out where we can see them now. I've never seen them like this before."

Ted ran toward them across the Deer Head. "What are you doing here?" he called.

Joey danced up and down with excitement. "We found the treasure," she shouted back, "and we came to find you."

She had the pleasure of seeing him really surprised.

"When?"

"Last night. At least we dug up a box we think might be the treasure, and we're going to open it as soon as you get there."

"Then let's hurry."

Ted took them through his own secret path, as he had the day they met him, at such a pace that Joey and Baptista were panting when they reached the house. The car was in the garage, so Joey guessed that Dad and the boys were back with Alex.

"In here," shouted Mac, hanging out the living-room window where he appeared to have been watching for them. "The Professor's all ready to start."

The living room looked a little like a schoolroom. The family was arranged in an attentive circle on chairs and stools. In the middle was the Professor, by a covered table on which sat the iron box and a neat group of tools, from keys to a crowbar. Alex stood beside him, holding the sewing-machine oil.

Joey and Ted dragged in three chairs from the dining room, and the latecomers settled themselves as near as possible.

"Oil," said the Professor seriously.

Joey tried not to laugh. Alex gravely handed over the little can. The Professor squirted the lock and selected a key. It didn't fit.

Next he probed the lock with a piece of wire. After a few minutes of careful study he took up another key, a very old carved one that came from Grandmother's collection. He gave the lock some more oil, and then, with the help of the wire, slowly twisted the key. Joey held her breath.

There was a gentle click. The Professor's face turned quite red with excitement. With shaking hands he reached out and raised the lid.

"Heck," said Donny angrily. "There's nothing there but cloth!"

Joey stared at the yellow linen that seemed to fill the little iron box. "There can't be!" she wailed.

But the Professor was smiling. "Wait!" His clever hands lifted the rotting material gingerly. Layer after layer seemed to crumble away, for all his care. And like a magician he waved triumphantly at a little brown book that appeared beneath the layers.

"That I am willing to wager is the diary and logbook of one Tom Bones, private gentleman, late of this coast. A very great find, I may say, very great."

"But where's the peacock?" Joey ran over to the table. The Professor seemed to have lost interest in everything except the little brown book, which he was turning caressingly in his hands. She dug her hands into the box and began pulling out the rotten cloth, ready to cry with disappointment. To find that Miss Betsy had taken the jeweled bird with her after all!

Her hands touched something hard. At the look on her face the twins, Ted, Alex, and Baptista crowded in to peer over her shoulder. And there they saw it, where it had lain for over a hundred years.

"It doesn't look much like a bird," said Baptista doubtfully.

"And it doesn't glitter like treasure," said Mac.

"But isn't it pretty!" Joey gave a deep sigh of satisfaction.

Dull gold, and fashioned of short, straight lines, the

only thing that made the object in the box look like a
peacock was its wide tail, trimmed with colored stones,
and its beaky little head with one purple eye. Joey
rubbed it gently.

"It may glitter when it's polished. I wonder if these
are rubies and emeralds."

"Early Aztec art." The Professor had turned the diary
over to Dad and was peering over her shoulder too.
"Our ancestors were often confused as to the value of
the 'jewels' they found in the New World. The Indians,
such as the Aztecs of Mexico who made this, cared only
for the color of stones, not their value as we think of it.
These are probably only semiprecious stones."

Joey tried to sort out this complicated and learned
speech. "You mean the jewels on the peacock aren't
worth a lot of money?"

"Precisely. However, it is a most interesting piece of
work and should find a home in any museum."

Joey put the bird to her cheek. When she held it she
could see the others who had held it before her. A dark-
skinned man, his feathered cape shining in the light of
a ceremonial fire. A red-kerchiefed ruffian, his earring
swinging in time to the swell of the black flag above
him. A slim girl in a gray dress, whose starched sleeve
rustled as she held the treasure to her cheek.

"I don't want the peacock to go to a museum," Joey
said fiercely.

"We'll have to find out who owns it before we start
deciding what's to be done with it," said Mom reasonably.

"Er-ah, after the interesting conversation on the trip
down with your grandmother, Joanna, I feel I can safely

say that the bird belongs to your family. Not only was it discovered on your land, but she was able to demonstrate conclusively that it is, indeed, a family heirloom."

Joey remembered Grandmother's explaining how they were descended from the Gray Gull Dudleys. And knowing Grandmother, Joey was sure that the ownership of the peacock was as good as proved.

"Good," she said happily.

Everyone set up a clamor to see this famous bird, and Joey passed it on. After Alex's turn, he sidled up to her, with a great smile cutting his face in half.

"Your father has spoken to my father about the school," he said. "I am to ride on the bus, which will pick me up every morning. All has been arranged."

Joey didn't see much to rejoice about in hearing you were going to school, but she knew that Alex's dearest dream had come true, so she was able to look pleased.

"I wish I were going with him," she thought sadly. Philadelphia and Grandmother were very close now. Even the joy of finding Miss Betsy's peacock couldn't overcome that dreadful happening.

Ted smiled at her gloomy face. "We'll be back together next summer," he said. "My brother may be home by then, and he'll show us some swell things to do."

"And you can come to see me in Philadelphia," added Baptista shyly.

Mac handed the peacock to Grandmother. "There's only one mystery we haven't solved," he said. "What happened to the bill of sale?"

Dad looked very red. "I'm afraid I have a confession to make." He was smiling his "guilty smile." "I took the bill of sale."

"Dad!"

"Why didn't you tell us?"

The children glared at him accusingly.

"So that's why you wanted to know where I put it. You even asked to borrow my atlas." Joey remembered now.

"I had an idea, and I didn't want anyone to be disappointed if it didn't work out," Dad explained.

Mom shook her head. "I hope you're planning to tell us now. It would be very sad for you to see your family pop with curiosity in front of your eyes."

"I had an idea," said Dad, "about studying local history with a view to clearing up some mysteries that show up in our national history. Joey had started down a trail that seemed to lead to big things, the problem of the legends of pirates along this coast, the study of the situation during the War of 1812. But most of all I wanted to find out what conditions were here many years ago. The dull little things that give historians the details of how people lived. What they paid for a pound of butter or a keg of rum."

Joey began to see the light.

"Dad!" she said accusingly. "You weren't even interested in our mystery. I bet I know what you wanted that bill of sale for. The prices on the other side!"

Professor Applegate seemed to think it was time to help Dad out. "And he's done a fine job. Already collected some valuable information—valuable."

"I wrote to the Professor when I had some work I thought he might be interested in seeing," Dad went on. "He kindly offered to come down here. And now I have the big surprise for everyone."

The eager silence would have pleased John Barrymore.

"He's asked me to work with him at his university near Philadelphia. I'll teach a class and do research this winter."

Mom began to smile.

"And so," Dad finished, "we're all going to live near Philadelphia this winter and come back to Holly River for the work on the bogs in the summer."

"Hooray!"

"Yippee!"

"Wa-hoo!"

"U-ah-uh-ah-uh-ahh!"

Dad nearly went down under the Indian-Tarzan dance of joy that took place around him. Mom kept shaking the Professor's hand, and even Grandmother was beaming.

"Won't we be going to Lawrenceville?" Mac asked suddenly.

"Oh yes," Dad said. "Joey and Mom and I will live in a house near the Professor's university, and you can visit us during your vacations. There's a very good school where we'll be living, and Joey will attend that."

Joey wanted to crow with happiness. It had been a wonderful summer after all. They had found the treasure and learned the secret that Holly River had hidden for over a hundred years. And, best of all, she had made three new friends.

She looked at their happy faces—dear Baptista, her first "best friend"; shy Alex, so nice and so funny in his strange little ways; and Ted.

"I like Ted most of all," Joey decided, "because he's part of Holly River, like the creeks and the swamps and the deer. And I love Holly River better than anything in the whole wide world."

"We'll be back next summer," she chortled. "All together! What do you suppose will happen then?"

And Grandmother, as usual, had the last word. "Humph!" said she.